Praise for
FANTÔMAS

"Absurd and magnificent lyricism."
Jean Cocteau

"Fantômas's great advantage over other heroes of popular literature is that he is evil incarnate— the reader will never suffer that unhappy moment when the villain hands the key to the story to an unappetizing representative of the law."
The New York Times Book Review

"Reading FANTÔMAS is like going on a roller coaster: you know what to expect but you scream, with fear and pleasure, anyway."
The Cleveland Plain Dealer

"A surreal work of art."
The New Yorker

THE SILENT EXECUTIONER

Being the Second in the Series of
Fantômas Adventures

Marcel Allain and Pierre Souvestre

Introduction by Edward Gorey

BALLANTINE BOOKS • NEW YORK

Library of Congress Catalog Card Number: 86-33112

ISBN 0-345-35297-1

This edition published by arrangement with William Morrow and Company, Inc.

Manufactured in the United States of America

First Ballantine Books Edition: February 1989

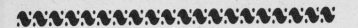

Contents

Introduction

by EDWARD GOREY

I tell you, Fantômas is alive!
I beg your pardon.
It's the last sentence of *Fantômas*.
Not surprising, really.
How do you mean?
Well, it is the first volume of a very long series, is it not?
Yes, thirty-two to be exact.
There you are.
Still, it makes you want to read the next.
Undoubtedly.

And now he has returned.
How can one be sure?
Of whom do you speak?
Of whom do you think?
I shudder to imagine.
Of whom else?

You cannot mean . . .
But I do . . .
Not . . . ?
Yes . . .
No, I cannot bear it.

Yes, I tell you.

Fantômas . . .

(Indescribable sensation)

How very jolly!

What have you there?

And to me, at least, quite unexpected.

With the lurid jacket?

The Silent Executioner.

Why your excitement?

It is the second of the Fantômas books.

Oh?

Oh, indeed! Perhaps this time the series will go on to the very end. . . .

It says it is a revised edition.

Revised?

Slang updated, and sentences omitted here and there for no discernible reason.

I hope the period flavor hasn't been destroyed.

I doubt if that would be possible.

Revised from what?

The Exploits of Juve.

Which was?

The original English translation that appeared in 1916–17 of *Juve contre Fantômas*, which had come out five years before.

Our grandparents or even our great grandparents seem to have been in no hurry.

No, but they persevered, for a time anyway. A dozen or so of the series were translated on the average of one a year until 1928.

But what is it all about?

Well may you ask.

Who is Juve?

He's—

Who is Fantômas?

He's—

Why are they against each other?

It's—

Will this second volume tell me?

In a way. Early on it contains a synopsis of the first.

But?

And it is, as they say in blurbs when there is every reason for disbelief, self-contained.

But?

Not really. I suggest you get *Fantômas*, available in hardcover and, even as we speak, also in paperback.

Besides, it has a delightful and informative introduction—

So different from this one. Clever of them.

—by John Ashbery that, among all sorts of other things, tells about the ongoing effect of Fantômas on French culture up until the present day.

What about American and English?

Since he doesn't mention it, I don't imagine there has been any to speak of.

Nothing at all?

I do remember with great pleasure, if not terribly clearly, a play by Richard Foreman with music by Stanley Silverman called *Hotel for Criminals*, which I saw in a sinisterly suitable mansion in the cultured wilds of western Massachusetts in the summer of 1974, and which could be described as based loosely on Fantômas . . .

You have digressed.

From what?

I'm not at all sure.

Why were you asked to write this introduction anyway?

I think perhaps because I may be almost the only other person (apart from Mr. Ashbery) known by name to be a Fantômas-addict.

And why are you that?

You might as well ask me why I am also an Oreo-addict.

All right, why are you an Oreo-addict?

That is rather mysterious in itself, considering that only seldom do they taste the way you think their Platonic archetype does, in spite of the fact that you would assume the recipe must be utterly impervious to fluctuations in the ingredients themselves.

Does that apply to the Fantômas books?

It just might.

There is of course a great deal of charm in a series, any series, and the longer the better.

You refer to a *roman-fleuve*?

Quite the contrary; not at all your Time like an ever-rolling stream/Bears all her sons away.

I don't follow.

True, it goes on and on, but the whole point is that it never gets anywhere at all. It is a marvel of treading water indefinitely.

I'm beginning to—

To put it another way altogether. Has anyone ever cared a button about Elsie Dinsmore as a grandmother?

Or again.

What now?

I can't help but throw out the notion that in his heyday Daffy Duck would have made a superb Fantômas, with Bugs Bunny as Juve, Melissa (from *The Scarlet Pumpernickel*) as Lady Beltham, and Elmer Fudd as Fandor.

The mind boggles.

Mine doesn't. Truly great inanity is hard to come by.

I'm leaving.

Before you go—

Yes?

Let me ask you a question.

Go ahead.

But were Juve and Fandor among the dead?

Not likely.

Clever you.

1
The Comrades' Tryst

"**A** pitcher of wine, Father Korn."
The raucous voice of big Ernestine rose above the hub-bub in the smoke-begrimed tavern.

"Some wine, and let it be good," repeated the drab, a big blonde with puckered eyes and features worn by dissipation.

Father Korn had heard the first time, but he was in no hurry to comply with the order. He was a bald, whiskered giant, and at the moment he was busily swilling dirty glasses in a sink filled with tepid water.

This tavern, the Comrades' Tryst, had two rooms, each with a separate exit. Mme. Korn presided over the first, in which food and drink were served. By passing through the door at the far end, and crossing the inner courtyard of the large seven-story building, the second den was reached—a low, dimly lit room facing the rue de la Charbonnière, a street known in the district for its unsavory reputation.

At a third summons, Father Korn, who had sized up the girl and the crowd she was with, growled, "It'll be two francs; hand over the stuff first."

Big Ernestine rose and, pushing her way to him, began a long argument. When she stopped to draw breath, Korn interposed.

"It's no use trying that line. I said two francs, and two francs it is."

"All right, I won't argue with a brute like you," replied the girl. "Everyone knows that you and Mother Korn are Germans, dirty Prussians."

The innkeeper smiled quietly and went on washing his glasses. Big Ernestine glanced around the room. She knew the crowd and quickly decided that the cash would not be forthcoming. For a moment she thought of tackling old Mother Toulouche, ensconced in the doorway, but she, snuggled in her old shawl, was fast asleep.

Suddenly from a corner of the tavern a weary voice cried with authority: "Go ahead, Korn. I'll stand them a pitcher."

It was the Sapper who had spoken, a man of fifty who owed his nickname to the report that he had spent twenty years in Africa, both as a soldier and as a convict.

While Ernestine and her friends hurried to his table, the Sapper's companion, a heavily built man, rose carelessly and slouched off to join another group.

"I'm too near the window here," he muttered.

"That's Nonet," explained the Sapper to Ernestine. "He's home from New Caledonia, and he doesn't care to show himself much just now."

The girl nodded and, pointing to one of her companions, became confidential. "Look at poor Mimile here. He's just out of the slammer and has to start right off to do his service. Pretty tough."

The Sapper became very interested in the conversation. Meanwhile, as he crossed the barroom Nonet stopped a few moments before a pretty girl who was obviously expecting someone.

"Waiting for the Square again, eh, Josephine?" he asked.

The girl, whose big blue eyes contrasted strikingly with her jet-black hair, replied, "Why not? Loupart isn't about to ditch me."

"Well, when he does, let me know," Nonet suggested with a smile.

Josephine shrugged contemptuously and, glancing at the clock above the bar, rose suddenly and left the room. She went rapidly down the rue de la Charbonnière and along the boulevard, in the direction of the Barbès metro station. On reaching the level of the boulevard Magenta, she slowed down and walked along the right-hand sidewalk toward the center of Paris.

"My little Jojo!"

The girl who, after leaving the tavern, had assumed a quiet, modest air, now came face to face with a stout gentleman with a jovial face and one gleaming eye, the other eye being permanently closed. He wore a beard that was turning gray, and his derby hat and light cane established him as a member of the middle class.

"How late you are, my adored Jojo," he murmured tenderly. "That accursed workshop been keeping you after hours again?"

Loupart's mistress suppressed a smile

"That's it!" she replied. "The workshop, Monsieur Martialle."

The man made a warning gesture.

"Don't mention my name here; I'm almost home." He pulled out his watch. "Too bad. I'll have to go in, or my wife will put up a stink. Let's see, this is Tuesday. Well, Saturday I'm off to Burgundy on my usual bimonthly trip. Meet me at the Lyons station, platform number two, Marseilles express. We won't be back till Monday. A delightful weekend of lovemaking with my darling, who at last consents . . . What's that!"

The man broke off his impassioned harangue as a beggar emerged from the darkness.

"Have pity on me, kind sir," the beggar implored.

"Give him something," urged Josephine.

The middle-aged lover complied and tenderly drew the pretty girl away, carefully repeating the details of the rendezvous.

"Lyons station; a quarter past eight. The train leaves at twenty to nine." Then, suddenly dropping Josephine's arm, "Now, sweetheart, you'd better hurry home to your good mother, and remember Saturday."

The outline of the portly personage faded into the night. Loupart's mistress shrugged her shoulders, turned, and made her way back to the Tryst, where her place had been kept for her.

At the back of the tavern the group that Nonet had joined

were discussing strange doings. The Beard, the leader of the gang known as the Cyphers, had just returned from the courthouse. He brought the latest news. Riboneau had been given ten years but was going to try for a reduced sentence. The talk suddenly stopped. A hubbub arose outside, a dull roar that grew louder and louder. The sound of hurrying footsteps mingled with shrill cries and curses. Doors were slammed. A few shots were fired, followed by a pause, and then the stampede began again.

Father Korn, deserting his bar, warily planted himself at the entry to his establishment, his hand on the latch of the door. He stood ready to block anyone who might try to force his way in.

"The raid," he warned in a low voice.

His customers, glad to be safe, followed the course of what to them was almost a daily occurrence. First came the frenzied rush of the streetwalkers, who, deserted by their sinister protectors, ran everywhere in search of shelter. Behind the shrieking herd the gendarmes, in close ranks, swept and cleared the street, leaving unsearched no corner, no court, no door, that remained ajar. Then the whirl swept away, the noise died down, and the street resumed its normal aspect: drab, weird, and alarming.

Father Korn laughed. "All they've bagged is Bonzville!" he cried, and the customers responded to his merriment. The police had been fooled again. Bonzville was a harmless old tramp who got himself nabbed every winter on purpose to lay up for repairs.

The roundup had caused enough stir in the barroom to distract attention from the entry at the back of a heavyset man with a bestial face, known as the Cooper.

He rushed to the Beard's table, and, taking the latter aside, began: "The big job is fixed for the end of the week. On my way back from the station I saw Josephine yakking with the customer. . . ."

Suddenly the Beard stopped him short. Everyone's attention had become fixed on the street entrance to the barroom. The door had opened with a bang, and Loupart, alias the Square, the lover of the pretty Josephine, came on the scene, his eyes gleaming, his lips smiling under an upturned mustache. Loupart was between two policemen who had stopped in the doorway.

The Square turned to them. "Thank you, gentlemen," he said in his most urbane voice. "I am very grateful to you for seeing me this far. I'm quite safe now. Let me offer you a drink to the health of authority!"

But the two policemen did not dare to enter the tavern, so they briefly declined and made off. Josephine had gotten up, and Loupart, after pressing a tender kiss upon her lips, turned to the company.

"That floors you, eh! I was just heading this way when I ran into the drive. As a peaceful citizen, I got hold of two cops and begged them to see me safely home. They thought I was really scared."

There was a burst of laughter. No one could bluff the police like the Square.

Loupart turned to Josephine. "How are things going, sweetie?"

The girl repeated her recent talk with M. Martialle in a low voice. Loupart nodded approvingly but grumbled when he found that the meeting was fixed for Saturday.

"Damn it! I'll really have to hustle with all the jobs on hand this week. Anyway, we won't let this one slip by. Plenty of dough, eh, Josephine?"

"You bet. He carries the stuff to his partners every two weeks."

"That's great, but in the meantime there's something doing tonight. Here, kid, get a pen and take down a letter for me."

The Square dictated in a low voice.

Sir, I am only a poor girl, but I've some feeling and honesty, and I hate to see wrong done around me. Believe me, you'd better keep an eye open on someone pretty close to me. Maybe the police have already told you I am the mistress of Loupart, alias the Square. I'm not denying it; in fact, I'm proud of it. Well, I swear to you that this Loupart is going to try a dirty swindle.

Josephine stopped writing.
"Look here, what are you up to?"

"Scribble, and don't worry about it. This doesn't concern you," replied Loupart dryly.

Josephine waited, docile and ready. But the Square's attention was now focused on Ernestine, her young man, and the generous Sapper.

"Yes," Ernestine was explaining to Mimile while the Sapper nodded approvingly, "the Beard is, as you might say, the head of the Cyphers, next to Loupart, of course. To belong to the Beard's gang you've got to have done in at least one guy. Then you get your number one. Your figure increases according to the number of stiffs you have to your credit."

"So then," said Mimile, with eager curiosity, "Riboneau, who has just been sentenced, is called number seven because . . ."

"Because," added the Sapper in his serious voice, "because he has killed off seven."

With a few curt questions the Square measured up young Mimile, who had impressed him favorably.

Josephine turned to Loupart. "What else should I put in the letter? Why are you stopping?"

As an answer, the Square suddenly sprang to his feet, seized a half-empty bottle and flung it onto the floor, where it broke. This act of violence sent the company scurrying, and Loupart roared: "It's on account of spies that I'm stopping! By God! When are we going to see the end of them? And besides," he added, staring hard at Ernestine, "I've had enough of all this nonsense. Better clear out of here or there'll be trouble."

Cunningly, with bloodshot eyes, her fists clenched in fury, but humbly submissive, the girl prepared to comply. She knew the Square was master, and there was no use resisting him.

The Sapper himself, unwilling to risk a brawl, growled, picked up his change, and, beckoning to his comrade, Nonet, effected a humble exit under cover of Ernestine.

Loupart's arm fell on Mimile's shoulder. He alone seemed to defy Josephine's formidable lover.

"Hold on," ordered Loupart. "You seem to have some nerve. Better join us."

Mimile's eyes lit up with joy.

"Oh!" he stammered. "Loupart, you'll take me into the Cyphers?"

"We'll see," was the enigmatic reply. With a shove he sent the young man to the back of the den. "Must go and talk it over with the Beard." Without paying any attention to the thanks of his new recruit, Loupart continued his dictation to Josephine.

As the Sapper and Nonet hurried down the rue de la Charbonnière, Nonet said: "Well, chief, what do you think of our evening?"

The individual whom the hooligans of La Chapelle knew by the nickname of the Sapper, and who was none other than Inspector Michel, slowly stroked his long beard.

"Not much," he declared, "except that we've been bluffed by the Square."

"Why not round up the bunch?" suggested Nonet, who was actually Inspector Léon.

"Talk is easy enough, but what can two of us do against twenty? You want to risk your neck for sixty dollars a month?"

In the meantime, Josephine was writing the Square's dictation:

> I know, sir, that tomorrow Loupart will be at Carnet's wineshop at seven o'clock, which you know is to the right as you go up the Faubourg Montmartre, before you reach the rue Lamartine. From there he will go to Doctor Chaleck's to tackle the safe, which is placed, I've been told, at the far side of the study, facing the window, with its balcony overlooking the garden. I wouldn't have meddled in the matter except that there'll be something worse regarding a woman. I can't tell you any more because this is all I know. Make the best of it, and for God's sake never let Loupart know the letter was sent to you by the undersigned.
>
> Very respectfully,

About to sign her name, Josephine looked up, trembling and anxious.

"What does it mean, Loupart? You've been drinking, I'm sure you have!"

"Sign, I tell you," replied the Square calmly. And the girl, hypnotized, proceeded to trace her name in her large, clumsy hand: "Josephine Ramot."

"Now put it in an envelope."

From the end of the bar the Beard was signaling Loupart.

"What is it?" the latter cried, annoyed at the interruption.

The Beard came near and whispered, "Important business. The dock man's scheme is going well—it'll be for the end of the week, Saturday at the latest."

"In four days, then?"

"In four days."

"All right," declared Josephine's lover, "we'll be on hand. It'll be a big haul, I hear."

"Fifty thousand at least, the Cooper told me."

Loupart nodded, waved the Beard aside, and resumed the dictation.

"Address it to Monsieur Juve, Commissioner of Safety, The Prefecture, Paris."

2
On the Track

The daily paper, *The Capital*, was about to go to press. The editors had handed over the last slips of copy with the latest news.

"Well, Fandor," asked the secretary, "nothing more for me?"

"No, nothing."

"You won't spring a 'latest' on me?"

"Not unless the president of the republic should be assassinated."

"Right enough. But don't joke. Lord, there's something else to be done just now."

The typesetter appeared in the editors' rooms.

"I want sharp type for one, and eight lines for two."

Discreetly, as a man accustomed to the business, Fandor withdrew on hearing the typesetter's request. He avoided the searching glance of the assistant editor, who, to meet the demands of the paging, immediately called one of the reporters at random and passed on the order to him.

"Some lines of special type—eight lines. Take up the Cretan question on the Havas telegrams. Be quick!"

Fandor picked up his hat and stick, and left the office. As a police reporter he was always on the move, his life completely unpredictable. He was never his own master, never knew ten minutes beforehand what he was going to do: whether he might go home, start on a journey, interview a

minister, or risk his life in an investigation of the world of
thugs and cutthroats.

"Damnation!" he cried as he passed the office door and
saw what the time was. "I've got to go to the courthouse,
and it's already very late." He ran forward a few paces, then
stopped suddenly. "And that porter murdered at Belleville! . . . If I don't cover that affair I won't have anything
interesting to turn in. . . ."

He retraced his steps, looking for a cab and swearing at
the narrowness of the rue Montmartre, which forced pedes-
trians onto the street. The street in turn was choked with fruit
and vegetable stands, buses, and that swarm of vehicles that
give Paris streets an air of bustle unequaled in any other capital in the world. As he was about to pass the corner of the
rue Bergère, a porter laden down with sample boxes strung
on a hook ran into him, almost knocking him down.

"Look where you're going!" cried the journalist.

"Look out yourself," replied the man insolently.

Fandor, shrugging his shoulders angrily, was about to move
on when the man stopped him.

"Sir, can you direct me to the rue du Croissant?"

"Follow the rue Montmartre and take the second turning
to the right."

"Thank you, sir. Could you give me a light?"

Fandor could not repress a smile. He held out his cigarette.
"Here, is that all you want today?"

"Well, you might offer me a drink."

Fandor was about to answer sharply when he was struck
by something vaguely familiar in the man's face. He was
about sixty. His clothes were threadbare and green with age,
his shoes run-down, his mustache and shaggy beard a dirty
yellow.

"Why the devil should I buy you a drink?"

"A good impulse, Monsieur Fandor."

In a moment the man's features seemed to change. He
appeared quite a different person, and Fandor recognized who
was speaking to him. Accustomed by long habit to concealing
his reactions, the journalist spoke nonchalantly.

"All right. Let's go to the Grand Charlemagne."

They started off together, reached the Faubourg Montmartre, and entered a small wineshop. After taking their seats and ordering drinks, Fandor turned to the porter.

"What's up?" he asked.

"It takes you a long time to recognize your friends."

Fandor scrutinized his companion.

"You are wonderfully made up, Juve."

On hearing his name mentioned, the man gave a start. "Don't mention my name! They know me here as old Paul."

"But why the disguise? Who are you after? Is it anything to do with Fantômas?"

Juve shrugged his shoulders. "Let's leave Fantômas out of it," he said. "At least for now. No, it's a very commonplace affair today, and I wouldn't have bumped into you except that I have an hour to while away and wanted your company."

"All this just for a commonplace affair?" cried Fandor. "Come, Juve, don't keep me in the dark."

Juve laughed at his friend's eagerness.

"You'll always be the same. When it comes to detective work, there's no keeping you out, is there? Well, here's the information you're after. Read that."

He passed Fandor a greasy, badly written letter. Fandor took it in at a glance.

"This refers to Loupart, alias the Square?"

"Yes."

"And you call it a commonplace affair? But look here, can you trust information given by a loose woman?"

"My dear Fandor, the police could not do without such tips, given for revenge by women of that class."

"Well, I'm going with you."

"No, I won't have you mixed up in this business; it's too dangerous."

"All the more reason I should be in it! What do you really know about this Loupart?"

"Very little, unfortunately," rejoined Juve. "And it's the mystery surrounding him that makes us uneasy. Although he's been involved in some of the worst crimes, he's always managed to escape arrest. He is supposed to be part of an organized gang. In any case, he's a resolute scoundrel who wouldn't hesitate to draw his gun in an emergency."

Fandor nodded.

"His arrest will make terrific copy."

"And for the pleasure of writing a sensational story you want to put your life in danger again!" Juve smiled sympathetically as he spoke. He had known the young journalist when, hardly grown-up, he had been involved in the weird affairs of Fantômas.

Fandor was an assumed name. Juve recalled the young Charles Rambert, victim of the mysterious Fantômas, the most redoubtable villain of modern times. He recalled the sensational trial and the terrible revelations that had appalled society. He had then affirmed a certain Gurn to be the lover of the Englishwoman, Lady Beltham. It was Gurn who had killed her husband, and Gurn was no other than Fantômas.

He recalled the tragic morning when Gurn, in the very shadow of the scaffold, had found a way to send an innocent victim in his place: Valgrand, the actor.

"When will you begin to draw in your net?" inquired Fandor.

Juve motioned to his companion to be silent and listen.

"Fandor, do you hear what that man's singing; the one drinking at the bar?"

"Yes, 'The Blue Danube.' "

"Well, that gives me the answer. We'll soon be on Loupart's tracks. By the way, are you armed?"

"If you won't run me in for carrying concealed weapons, I'll confess that Baby Browning is in my pocket."

"Good. Now, then, listen to my instructions. Loupart was seen at the markets this morning by two of my men, and you may be sure we haven't lost sight of him since. My reports indicate that he'll probably go to the Chateaudun intersection and from there to the place Pigalle, in the direction of Doctor Chaleck's house. We'll grab him at the intersection. Needless to say, we won't stay together. As soon as our man comes in sight you'll pass on ahead, keeping pace with him without turning around."

"And if Loupart doesn't appear?"

"Why then—" began Juve. "Listen! There's another customer whistling 'The Blue Danube.' It's time we got going."

"Are those your men whistling?" asked Fandor as they left the shop.

"No."

"What! Isn't it a signal?"

"It is, and you'll be able to find your trail by the passersby who whistle that tune."

While talking, the journalist and the detective arrived at the Chateaudun intersection. Juve glanced around.

"It's six o'clock. Get going, and prowl around Notre-Dame de Lorette. Loupart will probably come out of that wineshop over there to the right. You can recognize him easily by his height and the scar on his left cheek."

"Look here, Juve, why should these people whistle 'The Blue Danube' if they're not detectives?"

Juve smiled. "It's quite simple. If you whistle a popular tune in a crowd, someone is bound to take it up. Well, the two men I had watching out for Loupart this morning were whistling this same tune, and now we're meeting people who picked it up."

Fandor crossed the road and proceeded toward Notre-Dame de Lorette to the post the detective had assigned him. The manhunt was about to begin.

3
Behind the Curtain

The Cité Frochot is enclosed by low stone walls, topped by grating around which creepers intertwine. The entry to its main thoroughfare, shaded by trees and lined with small private houses, is not supposed to be public, and the porter's lodge to the right of the entrance is intended to enforce its private character.

It was about seven in the evening. As the fine spring day drew to a close, Fandor reached the square of the Cité. For the past hour the journalist had been completely absorbed in keeping track of the famous Loupart, who, after leaving the tavern, had sauntered up the rue des Martyrs, his hands in his pockets and a cigarette in his mouth.

Fandor allowed him to pass at the corner of the rue Claude, and from there kept him in view.

Juve had completely disappeared.

As Loupart, followed by Fandor, was about to enter the Cité Frochot, an exclamation made them both turn. Fandor could see a poorly dressed man anxiously searching for something in the gutter. A curious crowd had already gathered, and word was being passed around that the lost object was a twenty-five-franc gold piece.

Fandor, joining the crowd, was pushed close to the man, who quickly whispered: "Idiot! Keep out of the Cité."

The owner of the gold piece was none other than the de-

tective. Then, under cover of loud complaint, Juve muttered
to Fandor, "Let him go! Watch the entrance to the Cité!"

"But," objected Fandor in the same tone, "what if I lose
sight of him?"

"No chance of that. The doctor's house is the second one
on the right." The hooligan, who had for a moment drawn
near the crowd, was now heading straight for the Cité.

Juve went on: "In a quarter of an hour at the latest, join
me again—27 rue Victor-Massé."

"And if Loupart should enter the Cité in the meantime?"

"Come straight back to me."

Fandor was moving away when Juve addressed him out
loud. "Thank you, kind gentleman! But as you are so charitable, give me something more for God's sake."

Fandor drew near and Juve added, "If anyone questions
you as you pass through, say you are going to Omareille, the
decorator's; you'll find me on the stairs."

A few moments later the little crowd had melted away and
a policeman, arriving too late as usual, wondered what had
been going on.

Fandor carried out Juve's instructions to the letter. Hiding
behind a sentry box he kept an eye on the doctor's house, but
nothing unusual happened. Loupart had vanished, although
he was probably not far away. When the fifteen minutes were
up Fandor left his post and entered No. 27 rue Victor-Massé.
As he reached the third floor he heard Juve's voice.

"Is that you, lad?"

"Yes."

"The concierge didn't question you?"

"I've seen no one."

"All right, come up here."

Juve was seated at a hall window examining Doctor
Chaleck's house through a field glass.

"Has Loupart gone in?" he asked as Fandor joined him.

"Not while I was on watch."

"It's good to know one's Paris and have friends everywhere, isn't it?" continued Juve. "It occurred to me quite
suddenly that this might be an excellent place from which to
follow Loupart's doings. You would have spoiled everything

if you had followed him into the Cité. That's why I devised my little scheme to hold you back.''

"You are right," admitted Fandor, starting suddenly as Juve's hand gripped him hard.

"Look, Fandor! The bird is going into the cage!"

The journalist, excited, saw a familiar figure slipping into the little garden that separated Dr. Chaleck's house from the main thoroughfare.

The detective went on: "There he goes, skirting the house until he reaches the little door hidden in the wall. What's he up to now? Ah! He's fumbling in his pocket. False keys, of course.''

They saw Loupart open the door and go into the house.

"What comes next?" inquired Fandor.

"We're going to tighten the net the silly bird has hopped into,'' answered Juve. Bolting down the stairs, he added as a precautionary measure: "While I question the concierge, you slip by me into the main street. I have every reason to believe that Monsieur Chaleck has been away for two days. As soon as I get this information I'll pretend I'm leaving, and then . . . the rest is my concern.''

Juve's program was carried out to the letter.

To his questions the concierge replied, "Why, sir, I can't really say. I saw Doctor Chaleck go off with his bag, and I haven't seen him come back. However, if you care to see for yourself—''

"No, thanks," replied Juve. "I'll return in a few days. But look out, your lamp's flaring!''

As the concierge turned to see what was wrong, Juve, instead of going off to the right, quickly followed the direction Fandor had taken and caught up with him just outside Doctor Chaleck's house.

"Now for our plan of action," he said. "It's darker now than it will be later when the street lamps are lit and the moon's out. That excellent Josephine sent me a rough plan of the house. You see there are two windows on the ground floor on either side of the hall. Naturally they belong to the dining room and drawing room. The window to the right on the first floor is evidently that of the bedroom. The window on the left, with the balcony, belongs to the study of our dealer in death! That's where we must plant ourselves. Understand, Fandor?''

The journalist nodded. "I understand."

The two men advanced carefully, holding their breath and pausing at every step. To catch the thief in the act they must reach the study without giving the alarm.

The first story of Doctor Chaleck's house was only slightly raised above the ground. With the help of a drainpipe, Juve and Fandor managed to hoist themselves onto the balcony.

"What luck," cried Juve. "The study window is wide open!''

After Juve put on a pair of rubbers and Fandor removed his boots, the two men entered the room. Juve's first precaution was to test the two halves of the window. Finding that their hinges did not creak, he fastened the latch and drew the curtains.

"We'll risk a light," he whispered, taking out a flashlight. It lit up the room sufficiently to allow him to get his bearings.

The study was elegantly furnished. In the middle was a huge desk piled with papers, reports, and files. To the right of the desk in the corner, opposite the window and half hidden by a heavy velvet curtain, was the door leading to the landing. A large sofa took up the space of two wall panels. A set of bookshelves covered an entire wall. Here and there cozy armchairs invited meditation.

"I don't see the famous safe," murmured Fandor.

"That's because your eyes aren't trained," replied the detective. "Look at that corner sofa, topped by that richly carved bracket. Notice how thick the delicate mahogany panel seems to be. You can bet it hides a solid steel casket that even the best tools would have a hard job cutting through. That little molding you see to the right can easily be pushed aside.''

With the precision of an expert, Juve set the woodwork in motion and showed the astonished Fandor a scarcely visible keyhole.

"Now let's put out the light and hide behind the curtains. Luckily they're far enough from the window not to be noticed.''

For about an hour the men remained motionless. Then,

weary of standing, they squatted on the floor. Each had his revolver ready.

A distant clock struck ten, and suddenly a slight sound reached their attentive ears. The two had whiled away the time by drilling the curtains with a small penknife. These holes were invisible at a distance, but enabled them to see what was going on in the room.

The noise continued, slow and measured. Someone was walking about in the adjacent rooms without making any attempt to disguise the sound. Evidently Loupart believed he was quite alone in the doctor's house.

The steps drew nearer, and Fandor, in spite of his courage, felt his heart beating rapidly. The handle of the door leading from the hall to the study was turned, and someone entered the room.

There was a moment's silence, then the desk was suddenly lit up. The newcomer had found the switch. But he was not Loupart. He seemed to be a man of forty with a brown beard, brushed fan-shape; a noticeable baldness heightened his forehead, and a pair of bifocals were balanced on his strongly arched nose. Suddenly, having looked at the clock, which said half-past eleven, he began to loosen his tie and unbutton his waistcoat and then went out, leaving the study lit as if he intended to come back.

"It's Chaleck!" exclaimed Fandor.

"Just so," replied the detective. "And this complicates matters. We may have to protect him as well as his safe."

Indeed, Juve's first impulse was to go straight to Doctor Chaleck, apprise him of the situation, and, under his guidance, search the house thoroughly. But that would have put Loupart on the alert. It would be taking too great a chance. If Juve should lay hands on him outside of Chaleck's house he would have no right to hold him. The subtle power of Loupart lay in his remaining constantly a source of fear, always a suspect without ever being caught with the goods.

Coming back to his first idea of ensuring Chaleck's safety, Juve said to himself: "The doctor is coming back here, that's sure, and we must protect him without his knowing it. That is the best plan for the present."

Sure enough, after an absence of ten minutes Chaleck returned to the study and sat down at his desk. He had changed into his pajamas.

Time passed.

When the little Empire timepiece that decorated the mantel struck three, Fandor, for all his anxiety, could not repress a yawn. The night was long, and so far nothing out of the ordinary had happened. From their hiding place he and Juve kept an eye on Doctor Chaleck. When did the man sleep?

Nothing in the physician's countenance betrayed the slightest weariness. He examined numerous documents spread out on the desk, and also wrote a letter, which he sealed by lighting a candle and melting some wax. Afterward he lingered for a good twenty minutes, then finally put out the lights and left the room.

The room was now in total darkness. The journalist and the detective listened for a few minutes longer, but nothing happened to disturb the quiet of the night.

Half an hour more, and the outlines of the two men would be visible on the thin curtains. It was high time to go.

Fandor and Juve rose to their feet with difficulty; their legs had become cramped from the enforced rigidity.

"What now?" asked Fandor.

"Listen!" Juve gripped the journalist's arm as a new sound reached their ears. This time it was not the footsteps of a man walking carelessly but weird creakings, sly gropings. The noise stopped, began again, and again stopped. Where was it coming from?

"This room is a mass of hangings," muttered Juve. "It's impossible to locate or identify those sounds."

"You would suppose—" began Fandor.

But he stopped short. The door had opened, the light switched on, and Doctor Chaleck appeared once more, probably disturbed by the mysterious noises.

Chaleck gave a quick glance around the room. Then, to the dismay of the two men, he took a few steps toward the window, revolver in hand. At this point dull creakings could be heard, apparently from the landing. Chaleck turned quickly, and, leaving the door open, went out. Increasing light indicated that the other rooms in the house were being searched, and as the lights were gradually switched off again,

it became apparent that Chaleck was concluding his domicil-
iary investigation without having noticed anything abnormal.

The two men remained still for another hour, although they
had heard Chaleck go back to his room and lock himself in.
In the meantime, daylight was growing brighter, and in a
little while the neighborhood would be awake.

"We must slip out," said Juve as he turned the latch of
the window and, with infinite care, opened it to reach the
balcony. A few moments later he had shed his disguise, and
the two men caught their breath in the middle of the place
Pigalle, having fled ignominiously like common criminals.

4
A Woman's Corpse

"**W**ell, Juve, I suppose you'll agree with me that Josephine's information was a piece of pure fiction," said Fandor as they turned into the rue Pigalle.

"Nonsense," replied Juve.

"But," protested his companion, "we arrived punctually at the place appointed, and most assuredly nothing happened."

"Yes, we were punctual, but so was Loupart. Josephine's letter gave us two items of information: that her lover would be at Doctor Chaleck's house and that he would rob the safe. Events have proved her correct in one case. As for the second, while he did not break open the safe, there is no reason to think that was not his intention. He may have been frustrated by the unexpected appearance of Doctor Chaleck, or he may have discovered that we were following him."

At this moment Fandor pointed to three men who were running toward them, gesticulating violently.

"What's going on?" he asked.

"Why, it's Michel, Henri, and Léon!" Juve said. Then, turning to Fandor, he explained: "Three inspectors."

"Well, chief, what's up?" asked one of them.

"What do you mean?"

"You've just come from Cité Frochot, haven't you, chief?"

21

Juve was amazed. "Where have you come from, Michel? The prefecture?"

"No, chief, from the head office of the ninth arrondissement."

"Then how do you know we were at the Cité Frochot?"

Taken aback, Michel replied, "Why, from seeing you there after the affair."

"What affair?" insisted Juve.

"Well, chief, it was like this. The three of us were on duty this morning at the rue Rochefoucauld station. About twenty minutes ago the telephone rang and I heard a woman asking in a broken, choked voice if it was the police station. When I told her it was, she begged me to come to her rescue, crying, 'Murder! I'm dying!' "

"What then?" questioned Juve.

"Then I asked who was speaking, but unfortunately Central had cut me off."

"You made inquiries?"

"Yes, chief, and after a quarter of an hour Central told me that only one subscriber had called the police station—number 928-12, name of Doctor Chaleck in the Cité Frochot."

"I suppose you asked for the number again?"

"I did, but I got no answer."

After a pause, during which Juve was lost in thought, the officer added timidly: "We'd better hurry if a crime has been committed."

Juve beckoned to Michel.

"There are too many of us," he said. "You come along, Michel. You others go back to the station and be ready to join us in case you're needed."

The two officers and Fandor went hurriedly up the rue Pigalle, stopping at Doctor Chaleck's door. A loud ring brought no reply. It was repeated, and finally a voice cried: "Who is there? What's the matter?"

"Open," ordered Juve.

"To whom do you wish to speak?"

"To Doctor Chaleck." And Juve added: "Open, it's the police."

"The police! What on earth do you want with me?"

"You'll soon find out," answered Michel. "Do you suppose we'd be making this row if we were criminals?"

Apparently convinced by this reasoning, Doctor Chaleck finally decided to open his door.

"What do you want with me?" he repeated.

Juve quickly explained matters.

"We've just had a telephone message that some thieves, possibly murderers, are in your house."

"Murderers!" cried Chaleck in amazement. "But whom could they murder? I live here alone."

At this, Juve, Fandor, and Michel looked at each other, mystified.

"Well, in any case we must search your house from top to bottom," said Juve. As an afterthought he added, "I suppose you are thoroughly satisfied that we come with honest intentions?"

Doctor Chaleck smiled. "Oh! Inspector Juve's qualities are very well known to me, and I place myself entirely at his disposal."

The three men, led by Chaleck, searched all the rooms on the ground floor. Finding nothing suspicious, they then went upstairs.

"I have only three more rooms to show you, gentlemen," said the doctor. "My bathroom, my bedroom, and my study."

The bathroom revealed nothing of interest, and Chaleck, throwing open the door to another room, announced, "My study."

Fandor had hardly set foot in the study, from which he and Juve had so recently made their escape, when a cry burst from his lips.

"Good God! How horrible!"

The apartment had been completely ransacked. Overturned chairs bore witness to a violent struggle. One of the mahogany panels of the desk had been partly smashed in. A window curtain had been torn and left hanging, and the small gas stove was broken.

Fandor immediately saw what appeared to be a long trail of blood extending from the window to the desk. Stepping forward quickly, he discovered the body of a woman frightfully battered and covered with blood.

"Dead for some time," cried Fandor. "The body is cold and the blood already congealed."

Juve calmly examined the room, taking in its tragic horror. "The telephone is overturned," he muttered to himself. "The victim struggled with her murderer. Ah!—theft was the object of the crime."

"Theft!" cried Doctor Chaleck, coming forward.

"Look, doctor, your safe has been overturned, broken into and ransacked," answered Juve as he and Fandor cautiously lifted the woman. The body was a mass of contusions and appeared to be one big wound.

Juve turned to the doctor, who, livid with fear, was holding up a small gray linen bag that had contained his bonds.

"Try and stay calm, doctor. We need information. Can you make anything of it?"

"Nothing! nothing! I heard nothing. Who is this woman? I don't know her!"

Fandor pointed to a small shoe lying in a corner.

"A fashionable woman," he said.

"Yes," Juve replied. Putting his hands on Chaleck's shoulders, he said, "A friend of yours, a mistress, eh? Come now, don't deny it."

"Deny!" protested the doctor. "Deny what? You are not accusing me, are you? I know nothing about this, and, as you see, I have been robbed in the bargain."

"Is she a patient of yours?"

"I don't practice."

"A visitor, perhaps?"

"No one has been to see me today."

"Have you noticed this, sir?" interrupted Michel, as he handed Juve a handkerchief on which some viscous, grayish substance was spread in thick layers.

"Shoemaker's wax," Juve explained after a brief glance at it. "That explains the burns we noticed. The murderer covered his victim's face with the handkerchief to prevent identification." Then, turning to Fandor, he went on in a low voice: "But it doesn't explain how and when the crime was committed. Less than an hour ago we were in this very room, and cracking the safe alone would take a full hour."

Michel, ignorant of this fact, was all for arresting the doctor.

"Look here," he said to Chaleck sharply, "we've had enough of yarns from you; now tell us the truth."

"But, good God! I have told you the truth!" cried Chaleck.

"And you heard nothing, though you were only a few yards away?"

"Nothing at all. I sat up working very late last night. When I went to bed nothing the least bit suspicious had happened, except that toward morning I did hear a slight noise. I looked through the house, including this room, and found everything in order."

"That's a likely story!"

"It's true! Your ringing bell woke me not more than twenty minutes later, just as I was getting to sleep again."

"Lies!" cried Michel, turning to Juve. "Shall I arrest him?"

"The doctor is telling the truth," replied Juve, half regretfully.

Chaleck seemed relieved.

"Oh, you'll help me, won't you? Get me out of this abominable affair!"

As a matter of fact, Chaleck had accounted for his time with exact truthfulness.

Juve crossed the room and drew aside the curtains. On the floor were traces of mud. It was there that he and the journalist had stood.

"Doctor," said Juve at last, "I must ask you not to go out this morning. I am going to headquarters to ask them to send experts in anthropometry. We must photograph the appearance of your study in detail. Then I will come back and make an extended inquiry, and I shall want you. Michel, stay here with the doctor."

Without saying anything more, Juve, followed by Fandor, left the house, jumped into the first cab that passed and, mopping his forehead, cried: "It's astounding! This murder presents mysteries worthy of Fantômas himself!"

5

Loupart's Wrath

It was about ten in the morning, and along the rues de la Charbonnière, de Chartres, and Goutte-d'Or the women hawkers, driven from central Paris by the police, were heading for the shelter of the populous quarters.

Loupart strolled along the sidewalk, grabbing at the fruit stands and plucking a handful of strawberries or cherries as he went by. If the dealer happened to complain, she was quickly silenced by a word or a look.

The hooligan stopped at the Comrades' Tryst, in front of which Mother Toulouche had set out a table with a large basket of periwinkles.

"Want to try them?" suggested the old woman when she saw Josephine's lover.

"Hand me a pin," Loupart answered harshly, and in a few moments he had emptied a half-dozen shells.

"Friend Square, I've something to say to you."

"Out with it, then."

But before the old woman could reply, the sound of rollers coming down the sidewalk made her turn.

Loupart looked around with a smile. A cripple moving at an astonishing pace plumped into the basket of shellfish. The speed with which he traveled had earned him the nickname of the Motor. He was said to be an old railway mechanic who had lost both legs in an accident.

"Motor," cried Mother Toulouche, "I have to be away for ten minutes or so; look after my basket, will you?"

Following the old woman to her den Loupart entered with difficulty. The room was crowded with the loot of innumerable thefts all of which lay heaped pell-mell in this illicit bazaar.

Mother Toulouche, having shut the door, plunged into her subject.

"Big Ernestine is furious with you, Loupart."

"If she's threatening me," the hooligan replied, "I'll soon fix her."

"No, she didn't want to fight, but she was annoyed that you drove her from the Comrades' Tryst the evening before last for no good reason."

"For no good reason!" growled Loupart. "Then what was she doing with those spies, the Sapper and Nonet?"

"That can't be! Not the Sapper!"

"Spies, I tell you. They belong to headquarters."

The old receiver of stolen goods cast her eyes upward. "And they looked such decent people, too! Who can one trust?"

Loupart suddenly picked up a scarf pin set with a diamond and, tossing the old woman a five-franc piece, said as he left the room: "Tell Ernestine that I'm not mad at her."

Loupart had hardly gone a few steps along the rue de la Charbonnière when, at the corner of the rue de Chartres, he bumped into a passerby who was coming down the street.

Loupart burst out laughing. "What! Can this be you, Beard? What's happened to you?"

It certainly needed a practiced eye to recognize the famous leader of the Cyphers. The Beard, who owed his name to an abnormal hairy development, was clean shaven. In addition, he wore a soft, greenish hat and was dressed in a suit with huge checks.

"You told me to dress up like an American."

"I did, and you've made yourself look like a perfect hayseed. For heaven's sake, take it off. By the way, what about young Mimile?"

"He's with us."

"Well, what night do we pull it off?"

"Saturday night, unless the Cooper changes the time."
Loupart bent closer to his lieutenant.

"Is he—easy to recognize?"

"You can't miss him. Lean, dressed in dark clothes, and with one goggle eye."

Loupart touched the Beard's arm.

"First-class tickets for everybody."

"How many will there be?"

"Five or six."

"Women, too?"

"No, only my girl. But you can bet we won't be bored!" With these words Loupart walked away. A little later he stopped at the second house in the rue Goutte-d'Or, a decent-looking house with carpet on the stairs.

On reaching the fifth floor, he knocked several times on the door facing him, but there was no reply. This annoyed him. He didn't like Josephine to sleep late, and he expected her to be ready whenever he condescended to come and take her out.

Certainly Josephine had no reason to complain of her lover's conduct, and if at times he demanded blind submission, he never treated her with that fierce brutality that characterized most of his friends. But if Josephine had felt any leaning toward a straight life, or any scruples of conscience, she must have tossed them aside as soon as her relationship with Loupart began. With a different start in life she might have become an honest woman. But circumstances had made her the mistress of a gang leader, and, everything considered, she had a certain pride in being so, although she never took on the vulgar and brutal behavior of her companions.

At the third knock Loupart, none too patient, pushed the door in with a vigorous shove of his shoulders.

Josephine's apartment, a comfortable and spacious room, with a fine, bird's-eye view of Paris, was empty. Assuming his mistress was gossiping at some neighbor's, he bawled: "Josephine! Come here!"

Heads appeared, anxiously looking out of other rooms on the floor.

"Where is Josephine?" Loupart cried.

Mme. Guinon came forward.

"I don't know," she replied, stammering. "She complained of pains in her stomach last evening, and I was told she's gone."

"Gone? Gone where?" stormed Loupart.

"Why, I don't know. It was Julie who told me."

A freckled face appeared, half hidden by a matted shock of hair. Julie wasn't reticent like her mother. She explained in a hoarse, alcoholic voice.

"It's simple. When I came in last night about four I heard groans in Josephine's room. I went to look and found Josephine writhing in pain—as if she'd been poisoned."

"What did you do then?"

"Oh, nothing," declared Julie. "It wasn't my business, but the Flirt came and meddled in it."

"The Flirt! Where is she?"

The Flirt, a faded, wrinkled woman of fifty, appeared from a doorway where she had been listening.

"Where is Josephine?" demanded Loupart.

"At Lâriboisière Hospital; ward twenty-two, if you want to know."

After a moment's amazement Loupart broke out furiously: "You sent Josephine off in the middle of the night! You took her to a hospital for a little indigestion! Without asking me? Why, she's no more ill than I am!"

"Have to think she is," replied the Flirt, "since she's still there."

Loupart turned and stomped downstairs swearing. "She'll come out of there a damned sight quicker than she went in!"

A few minutes later he entered Father Korn's bar. Having told that worthy gentleman of his plans, Loupart listened as they were demolished.

"You can't do anything today, so there's no use trying. You'll have to wait till the visiting hour, tomorrow afternoon."

Loupart grudgingly acknowledged the truth of the bar-owner's assertion and, calling for writing paper, sat down and scrawled a letter to his mistress.

"Motor," he cried to the cripple who was still watching Mother Toulouche's basket, "tumble along with this note to

Lâriboisière. Look sharp, and when you get back I'll buy you a drink.''

As the cripple hurried away he was all but knocked down by a newsboy, running and shouting: ''Extra! Extra! Get *The Capital*. Extraordinary and mysterious crime of the Cité Frochot. Murder of a woman.''

''Shall I get a copy?'' asked Father Korn.

Loupart stalked out of the bar without turning.

''Oh, I know all about that,'' he cried.

Father Korn stood rooted to the spot at Loupart's answer. ''What! He knows already!''

6
The Lâriboisière Hospital

T he clerk, who had admitted Juve, withdrew, and M. de Maufil, the director, gave the police officer his most gracious smile.

"When I asked for an officer, I hardly expected to be sent such a celebrated detective for a matter that is really very commonplace."

"Your letter to Monsieur Havard mentioned someone I have been looking for with the greatest interest for the past two days: Loupart, alias the Square. That is why I came myself," replied Juve. "What is it about, sir?"

"Well, the day before yesterday we admitted a patient suffering from acute gastric trouble. The woman identified herself as Josephine Ramot, no calling, residing in Paris, rue Goutte-d'Or, in furnished rooms. Several hours after her admission to the hospital, she received a letter, brought by a messenger, that threw her into a violent state of agitation. The nurse on duty sent for me, and I succeeded, after great difficulty, in quieting her. But she insisted on leaving the hospital at once. The poor creature had a high fever, and to grant her request would have been sending her to her death. She finally gave me the letter that had excited her so. Here it is; kindly look it over."

Juve took the letter and read:

Am just back from the flat. You ain't there, and I don't

31

want no more of these dodges. You are no more ill than I am. You either leave the hospital and hightail it back to the house right now or tomorrow, Friday, at visiting time, as sure as my name's what it is, you'll get two bullets in your hide to teach you to hold your tongue.

Juve gave a grunt of satisfaction.

"You understand what is going on?" asked the director.

"Yes, but please go on with your story."

"Well, sir, you can guess that having read this letter, I went to the girl for information on the writer. According to what she told me, this Loupart is her lover, and the girl is convinced that tomorrow he will come and kill her."

"You've told her that all precautions will be taken?"

"Of course. I pointed out to her that people do not come in here as they do into a bar; that being warned, I will have all the visitors watched who come here and ask to see her. I repeated to her that her lover probably wanted to frighten her but that he could not do anything to hurt her. I insisted that in her condition it was physically impossible for her to leave."

"And what was her answer to that?"

"Nothing. Her agitation having subsided, she seemed to fall into a condition of extreme prostration. It was obvious that she had a far higher opinion of Loupart's daring than of my watchfulness and that she regarded herself as condemned. She stayed only because she realized that it was out of the question for her, in her weak state, to go back home."

While the director spoke, Juve kept smiling, a satisfied expression on his face. He seemed unconcerned about Josephine. "Tell me, inspector," the director continued, "what is this all about?"

Juve hesitated, then said: "It would take too long to recount the motives that prompted Loupart to write that letter. This Josephine whom you see today trembling at her lover's threat not so long ago supplied the police with valuable information concerning him. Perhaps he has found out somehow. Did he fear, above all, that she would tell tales again here at the hospital? It is quite possible. You see, he must have had very strong reasons for giving her the order to come home—"

Juve broke off here, fingering Loupart's letter. Finally he placed it in his pocket.

"I will keep this document, director. It is tangible proof of Loupart's criminal intentions. If he should try to carry out his threats now, it would be difficult for him to deny premeditation."

"You think that such a thing is possible?"

"Don't you?"

"Loupart says he will come to the hospital before three and kill his mistress, but surely it is not difficult to stop him."

"You think the police are all-powerful, that we can arrest would-be murderers and render them harmless? That is a misconception. A swarm of regulations prevent us from taking effective action. If I met Loupart on the street I'd have no grounds to arrest him. When a man holds his life cheap and is determined to risk everything, he has a pretty good chance of succeeding. Of course I shall take every measure to prevent Loupart from killing his mistress, but I'm not at all sure of success."

"But, Monsieur Juve, we must have this girl transferred to another hospital if necessary."

Juve shook his head.

"And show Loupart we are aware of his intentions? No, we must let him come, and catch him as he is about to commit the crime."

"What do you propose to do?"

"Study the hospital; arrange where to place my men," replied Juve.

"In that case I'll do everything I can to help you." M. de Maufil rang for an attendant and asked him to take Juve to Doctor Patel's department.

Juve thanked the director and left. The attendant pointed to a row of windows under the roof.

"The girl is under the care of Doctor Patel. His section begins at the corner window and runs to the window near the cornice."

"How can the women's ward be reached?"

"Either by the door on the staircase or by the door at the back, which leads into the laboratory of the head physician, the room of the house surgeon on duty, and the departmental offices."

"And how do visitors get in?"

"Visitors always go up the main staircase."

"Now," said Juve, "show me Doctor Patel's section."

"Very good, sir. It will be all the more interesting to you, as he is now on his rounds."

When Juve entered the women's ward, Doctor Patel was already in the process of seeing his patients. He was passing from bed to bed, questioning each of the women under treatment and listening to the comments of the house staff who followed him.

"Gentlemen," the doctor was saying as Juve joined the group, "the patient we have just seen is a typical example of intermittent fever. The serum tests have not given any definite result; it is therefore impossible to arrive at—"

A hand was laid on Juve's shoulder.

"Why, the tests are always absolutely indicative! Palpable typhoid, eh? What do you think?"

Juve turned his head and could not suppress a cry of surprise.

"Doctor Chaleck!"

"What! Monsieur Juve! You here! Were you looking for me?"

Juve was dumbfounded. He drew Chaleck aside.

"Then you're attached to this hospital?"

"Oh, I only have permission to attend the courses."

"And I came here out of curiosity."

"In any case, allow me to thank you for coming to my rescue the other day. The officer who was with you seemed to take me for the guilty man."

"Well, you see, appearances . . ."

"But if anyone was a victim it was I. Apart from the murdered woman being found in my house, I have been robbed!"

Here the doctor broke off. A house surgeon was beckoning to him.

"Forgive me," he said to Juve. "I cannot keep my colleague waiting."

Leaving Chaleck, Juve went back to the attendant, who was patiently waiting for him.

"Stranger than ever!" he thought. "There is no making it all out. Josephine writes that Loupart means to rob Chaleck. I track Loupart, and he gives me the slip. I spend a night in a room where I see nothing, but where, nevertheless, a horrible crime is committed. The murder takes place barely a yard away from me, and the doctor, the tenant of the house, sees nothing either, and does not even know the victim, who is found next morning on his premises! Thereupon our informant, Josephine, goes into the hospital. Pain in the stomach, they say—hem! Poison, maybe? Then she gets a threatening letter from Loupart. And when I come to the hospital to protect her, whom should I meet but Doctor Chaleck!"

Juve, turning to the attendant who was escorting him, asked, "Do you know the person I was speaking to just now?"

"Doctor Chaleck? Yes, sir."

"What is his business here?"

"He is a foreign doctor. Belgian, I think. Anyway, he is allowed by the authorities to follow the clinical courses and do research in the laboratory."

7

A Revolver Shot

There was unusual commotion in Doctor Patel's section that afternoon. Not only were the patients allowed to receive visitors, but quite a number of strange doctors had spent the day going from bed to bed, notebooks in hand, studying the patients and their temperature charts. The nurses hesitated to call these individuals doctors, and the patients, too, seemed aware of their true status. Whispers were hushed, and all eyes turned toward the far end of the ward.

There, in a bed slightly apart and near the house staff's quarters, lay Josephine, racked by a high fever and breathing with difficulty. Just opposite her was an old woman who had been admitted that morning. Her face was almost entirely hidden under voluminous bandages.

As the ward clock struck a quarter to three, an attendant appeared and announced: "In ten minutes visitors will be requested to leave."

Two of the staff, who had paced the ward since early in the day, exchanged a smile.

"Here's the end of the farce," remarked one; "Loupart isn't coming."

"He said three; there are still thirteen minutes left," replied the other.

"Well, every precaution is being taken."

"Precautions are useless with men like Loupart."

"Eleven minutes left."

"What the devil could happen? Visiting hour is over; the visitors are leaving."

"Three minutes!"

"Look here, you'll end by making me think . . ."

"Two minutes."

"Well, admit you're wrong!"

"One minute."

Suddenly two shots rang out, startling the silent ward. The patients leaped from their beds and sought refuge in the corners, while the two house surgeons and the policemen, disguised as doctors, rushed in a body toward Josephine's bed. Doors slammed. People hurried from every direction.

A calm voice rose above the hubbub. "What the devil! I'm drenched! What does this mean?"

The house surgeon reached the bed where the hopeless Josephine lay, white as a corpse, motionless. A large red blood stain was spreading on her sheet. The doctor quickly uncovered the wounded woman and examined her.

"Fainted, she has only fainted!" And, silencing all comments, he called: "Monsieur Juve! Monsieur Juve!"

The old woman who, a few moments before, had been dozing, now sprang out of bed, and, tearing off her bandages, revealed the features of Detective Juve.

"I understand everything except why I'm drenched to the bones," declared Juve as he crossed over to Josephine's bed, oblivious to the sensation his appearance had created.

"That's easily explained," said the house surgeon. "The girl was lying on a rubber mattress filled with water. One of the bullets punctured it."

"Was she injured?"

"A contusion on the shoulder. The murderer aimed badly owing to her recumbent position."

Juve beckoned to the officers.

"Your report? You've seen nothing?"

"Nothing."

"That's strange," declared the detective. "I kept an eye on Josephine myself, thinking that some movement on her part would betray the entrance of Loupart. She made no sign. But however Loupart may have got in, he can't get out without falling into a trap. I have fifty men posted around the building. Now, the first point to clear up is the exact location from which the shots were fired."

"How can we get at that?"

"Very simply. By drawing an imaginary line between the spot where the bullet struck the mattress and where it went into the floor—extend this line and we find the spot from which the shot was fired." A doctor came forward.

"Monsieur Juve," he said, "that would bring us to the door of the staff room."

"Ah, it's you, Doctor Chaleck! I'm glad to see you! You are quite right. Do you see any objection to my reasoning?"

"I do. I came into the ward barely two seconds before the gunshots were fired. There was no one behind me, and no one in front of me."

Juve crossed over to the door.

"The shots were fired from here!" And as he stooped and picked up an object from the floor, the detective added triumphantly: "And this proves it!"

He held out a revolver, still loaded in four chambers. "A precious bit of evidence!" He turned to the doctor. "Can a stranger get into the wards by this door?" he asked.

"It is utterly impossible, Monsieur Juve! Only those thoroughly familiar with Lâriboisière can get into the ward through the laboratory. You must pass through the surgical departments."

The detective sat at the foot of the sick woman's bed and mechanically laid the revolver beside him. But he had hardly done so when he sprang up. On the sheet was a tiny red speck left by the muzzle of the weapon.

"Ah! That's very instructive!" he cried. And as the others crowded around, puzzled, Juve added: "Don't you see? The murderer ran his finger along the barrel to steady his aim, and since the barrel is very short, the bullet grazed the tip of his finger, which extended slightly beyond it. If I find anyone in the hospital with a wounded finger, I've got the murderer! Gentlemen, I am going to ask the director to issue orders for everyone within the hospital gates to pass before me. Within two hours at the most, the culprit will be in our hands."

* * *

The attempted murder took place at three o'clock. By about six o'clock, those who had first been examined by Juve had received permission to leave the hospital and were beginning to depart.

Doctor Chaleck headed for the exit that he used every evening when leaving Lâriboisière. As he was about to pass through the door, a police officer blocked his way.

"Excuse me, sir. Have you a pass?"

"A pass?"

"Yes, sir. No one is allowed to leave today without a pass from Monsieur Juve."

The doctor looked at his watch.

"Damn," he said. "I'm late as it is. Where am I to get this pass?"

"You must ask Monsieur Juve himself for it. He is in the director's private room."

"All right, I'll go there." And Doctor Chaleck retraced his steps.

8
The Search for
the Criminal

"I t's astounding!" declared M. de Maufil. "We have already examined nearly two hundred people and still we've found nothing."

"That may be," replied Juve, "but the culprit may be the two hundred and first hand held out to us."

"You're forgetting one thing, Monsieur Juve."

"What's that?"

"If the culprit gets wind of our method of investigation, he won't be stupid enough to submit to your inspection."

Juve nodded approval.

"You're right. And I've anticipated that problem."

Since he had begun his inquiry on the spot, from the very moment the revolver shots had rung out, the great detective had grown more and more certain that the arrest of the mysterious offender would take a considerable amount of time. The buildings of the hospital were extensive, and it would be easy for a man to move about them without attracting attention. They offered unusual opportunities for hiding.

"Monsieur Director," said Juve, "I imagine we have inspected just about everyone who usually leaves Lâriboisière at this time."

"That is so."

"Then we must now change our plan. We can leave a nurse here to detain those who come to ask for passes, and begin

40

a search of the hospital ourselves. I will post my officers in line, each man keeping in sight the one behind and the one before him. I will leave an officer at the foot of every staircase. Then, beginning at the outer wall of the building, we will drive everyone on the ground floor toward the other end. If we don't round up our man there, we will proceed to the floor above.''

When Doctor Chaleck found that the inspector watching the exit leading to the main door in the rue Ambroise-Paré refused to allow him out of the hospital without the permission of the great detective, he had to retrace his steps. Skirting the bushes in the courtyard, he went toward the medical wards, turning his back on the administrative offices, where he might have encountered our friend Juve. He had taken off his white uniform and was dressed in his street clothes. He stopped at the entrance to the long gallery that extends to the operating rooms of the surgical department. Turning suddenly, he could see Inspector Juve in the distance, coming his way and accompanied by the director. At the same time he noticed the cordon of officers preparing to sweep the hospital from end to end. Mechanically, and as if bent on putting a certain distance between himself and the newcomers, he turned into the gallery. Reaching the far end, he was about to go into the surgical ward when a nurse stopped him.

"Doctor, you can't go in just now. Professor Hugard is operating, and he has given express orders that no one is to be admitted.''

Chaleck turned up the gallery again but abruptly swung around as he caught sight of Juve and the director just entering the gallery, shepherding before them a half-dozen patients and orderlies. Chaleck joined this little group, which had pulled up at the end of the gallery and was making amused comments about the inspection to which they were about to submit.

"Now's the time to show clean hands,'' joked an intern. "Eh, Miss Victorine?'' he added, smiling at a buxom nurse.

"Depend on it,'' growled one of the accountants of the administrative department, shrugging. "They're making a big fuss over nothing. After all, no one is hurt. Just one more pistol shot. Who counts them in this neighborhood?''

An old man, who had his hand bandaged, suggested: "Perhaps they'll be wanting to arrest me since the culprit is wounded in the fingers, they say."

Dignified and calm, Juve did his best to quickly release each person brought to him. They had only to show their two hands held in front of their faces, the fingers apart. M. de Maufil, at a sign from Juve, immediately gave the attendant the go-ahead to provide the person in question with a card bearing his name and description. Armed with this "Sesame," he could come and go all over the hospital unimpeded.

Pointing to a large door at the extreme end of the corridor, Juve asked, "What exit is that?"

M. de Maufil smiled. "You want to see everything, don't you?"

Opening the heavy door, the director made room for Juve, who entered a narrow passage that was damp and dark. The passage, a short one, opened on a vast room, much like a cellar, lighted by vents in the ceiling and intensely cold. The sound of running water from open taps broke the silence of the place, whose only furnishing was a huge slab of wood running from one end of the room to the other. On the slab dim white shapes were outstretched, and when his eyes grew accustomed to the twilight, Juve recognized the vague outline of these weird bundles. They were corpses swathed in shrouds. Only the heads and shoulders were visible, and on the brows of the dead icy water trickled, dispensed sparingly but regularly by duck-billed taps that were suspended over an inclined surface.

"This is the amphitheater where we keep the bodies for postmortems," the director explained. "Do you want to stay any longer?"

"There is no access to the room except by the door through which we came in?"

"None."

"In that case," said Juve, "and as there is no furniture here for a person to hide in, let's look elsewhere. It is a rather gruesome place."

"You're not used to the sight, that's all," replied the director as he led the way back to his office.

Juve looked at his watch. "Well, I must leave you now and report to Monsieur Havard. I'm afraid the murderer has slipped through our fingers."

"But you'll come back?"

"Of course."

"What should I do in the meantime?"

"Nothing, unless you care to go over the hospital again."

"And the passes? Are they still to be enforced? We have no one in the place but the staff."

"That is essential," replied Juve. "I must know with certainty who comes in and goes out. However, anyone known to your doorkeeper who wishes to leave need only sign a register."

9
In the Morgue

It was light in the evening. One by one the rooms in Lâriboisière were being lit up. The only exception was the grim amphitheater, whose occupants would never need to see again.

Suddenly—and if anyone had been present, he would have had the most frightening experience it is possible to conceive—a corpse stirred.

Having assured himself that the door between the amphitheater and the gallery was shut, the corpse, shivering with cold, threw off the shroud that had enveloped him, and set to work moving his arms and legs to get the circulation going again. At the far end of the room, this living corpse discovered, under a zinc basin attached to the wall, a bundle of linen and garments, which he seized. His body shaking with cold, the man dressed himself in haste, and then waited until he thought his clothes were sufficiently dry not to attract attention.

Making sure the gallery was deserted, he came out and walked rapidly to the courtyard. To the right of the main gate, the smaller gate leading into the rue Ambroise-Paré was open. The man passed under the archway, and in a moment would have been clear of Lâriboisière, but the porter blocked his way.

"Excuse me, who goes there?" Then, having looked more closely: "Why it's Doctor Chaleck! You're late leaving us

44

this evening, doctor. I suppose you've been kept pretty busy
in ward twenty-two?''

"Yes," replied Chaleck. "That's why I'm in a hurry,
Charles.''

And Chaleck, with an impatient gesture, was about to slip
out when the porter stopped him again.

"One moment, doctor; you must sign out first."

"Is this a new hospital regulation?"

"No, doctor. The police have ordered everyone entering
or leaving the hospital to sign his name in this book.''

The porter, having taken Doctor Chaleck into his lodge,
opened a new register and, pointing to a half-dozen names
already written on the first page, added: "You won't be in
bad company; you're to sign just below Professor Hugard."

Chaleck smiled. "Tell me the latest news, Charles. Do
they suspect anyone?''

"All I know is that fifty of them came here with dirty
shoes, made a hubbub around the patients, upset everything,
and in the end caught nobody at all. But if the culprit is still
here, he won't get out without the bracelets on his wrists!''

An equivocal smile touched Chaleck's pale lips. It might
be that the mysterious inhabitant of the little house in the
Cité Frochot did not share the porter's confidence in the
shrewdness of the police. Perhaps he was thinking that a few
hours earlier, a certain Doctor Chaleck, hemmed in a passage
with no exits and about to be compelled to show, like everyone else, the tips of his fingers, had, under the nose of the
officers, and even of the artful and astute Juve, suddenly vanished—gone out of the world of the living—and thought it
necessary, for reasons he alone knew, to assume the rigidity
of a corpse, the stillness of death. But in a moment the smile
had become frozen.

The doctor, who had kept both hands in his pockets while
talking to the porter, suddenly felt a sharp twinge in the fingers of his right hand, and it became moist and lukewarm.
This happened as the porter held out the register for him to
sign.

"Charles," he cried, "I'm in a great hurry. While I'm
signing, please go out and stop the first taxi that passes.''

"Certainly, sir," replied the man.

The porter had barely turned his back when the doctor drew out his right hand and with evident difficulty began to write, holding the pen between the third and fourth fingers, as though unable to use the others.

As he was finishing his entry, he made what was apparently an involuntary movement. Something unexpected happened, because he suddenly turned pale and swore under his breath. Charles was just coming back to the lodge.

"Your taxi is here, Doctor."

"Right. Thank you."

Chaleck closed the register abruptly, jumped into the car, and threw an address to the driver, who got under way. On seeing the doctor shut the register, Charles cried: "The devil—there's no blotting paper in it; it will be sure to smear!"

And though it was too late, the porter rushed to the book and opened it. His eyes became fixed on the page where the signatures were. He stared, wide-eyed.

"Oh! Oh!" he murmured.

10
The Bloody Signature

M. de Maufil was exceedingly nervous.

"As soon as you went back to headquarters," he declared to Juve, some moments after that officer had been shown into his private room, "I continued the search with redoubled efforts. Neither the ward nurses, in whom I place complete confidence, nor the heads of my staff, whom I have known for many years, exited the doors of the hospital. In fact, I took every precaution and obeyed your instructions to the letter—yet all in vain."

"You found nothing?"

"Nothing. Not even a trace of him."

"That's strange."

"It's maddening. It would seem that from the instant the man fired those two shots in the women's ward in Patel's department, he vanished. Your notion of examining the hands of everyone in the hospital was an excellent one, but nothing came of it.

"He must have known the snare we were preparing for him and didn't turn up at the hopsital exit, so we must conclude that he is still inside the gates, hidden in some remote corner, or underground. However, the first thing to do is protect the girl Josephine. She saw nothing, I suppose?"

"She says she did not see Loupart come in, but she insists

47

with a sort of perverse pride that it must have been Loupart who fired at her because he threatened to do so."

A knock at the door was followed by the timid entrance of the porter.

"Is that you, Charles? Come in," called the director. "What do you want?"

"It's about the signature, sir. There is blood on my book."

In a moment Juve had leaped from his chair and torn the register out of the man's hands.

"Blood!"

He turned the pages feverishly until he came to the writing. Without waiting for de Maufil's permission, he dismissed the porter.

"Very good, I'll talk to you in a little while."

The door had barely shut when Juve pointed to the page. "Look! Doctor Chaleck's signature! And just below it this mark of blood! What do you say to that, sir?"

"But it's sheer madness. Chaleck couldn't be guilty!"

"Why not?"

"Because I know him. He was recommended to me seven months ago by an old comrade of mine. Chaleck is a man of brains, a foreign physician, a Belgian. He's here specially to study intermittent fevers. Monsieur Juve, I tell you he has nothing whatever to do with this affair."

Juve picked up his hat and stick. He was restless and uneasy. The director's outburst had not greatly impressed him.

"Doctor Chaleck could not explain how his finger came to be hurt, and he did not inform us of the fact."

"A mere coincidence."

"Possibly, but it is a terrible coincidence for him," replied Juve.

On leaving the director's room, the detective couldn't help rubbing his hands. "This time I have him!" he muttered. He went down the stairs quickly, crossed the great courtyard of the hospital, and proceeded to knock at the porter's lodge.

"Tell me, my friend, precisely what happened when Doctor Chaleck left the hospital?"

With much detail, for he now felt very proud of having played a part in the affair, the worthy man related how Doctor Chaleck had come to the gate, sent him after a cab while signing his name, then made off, after having, no doubt by an oversight, closed the register.

"Very good! Thank you," Juve said, giving the man a generous tip.

This time he was leaving Lâriboisière for good.

"Very characteristic, that piece of impudence," he reflected. "Very like Doctor Chaleck, that device of shutting the register he had just stained with blood in order to give himself time to get away!" On reaching the boulevard Magenta he hailed a cab.

"Rue Montmartre. Stop at *The Capital*. You know it?"

A few minutes later Juve was shown into Fandor's office. But the detective was no longer smiling, and his air of abstraction did not escape his friend.

"Anything fresh?" inquired Fandor.

"Much that is fresh! That's why I came to see you."

The detective proceeded to tell the reporter the startling discovery he had just made at Lâriboisière.

"There," he said. "I suppose you can turn that into a thrilling story, eh?"

"I certainly can."

"The arrest is now just a matter of time."

"And how are you going to go about it?"

"I don't quite know. Well, good-bye."

Fandor let the detective reach the door of the office, then called him back.

"Juve!"

"Yes?"

"You are hiding something from me."

"I? Nonsense."

"Yes," persisted Fandor. "You are concealing something. Don't deny it. I know you too well, my friend, to be content with your reticence."

"My reticence?"

"You didn't come here merely to give me copy."

"Why—"

"No. You had another reason for looking me up, then you changed your mind. Why?"

"I assure you you are mistaken."

Fandor rose.

"All right, if you won't tell me I'll have to follow you."
At the journalist's announcement Juve shrugged his shoulders.

"That's what I was afraid of. But it's absurd to be always
dragging you into risky affairs."

"Where are we going?" asked Fandor briefly, lighting a
cigarette.

"We are going to Doctor Chaleck's. If he's there we will
force a confession from him; if he's not there, we will ransack his house for clues—like good burglars!" Juve added,
"I have a whole bunch of false keys. We'll be able to get
into Doctor Chaleck's without ringing the bell. Here's a snapshot I took of Josephine at the hospital." Throwing the evidence on Fandor's desk, he said, smiling, "Not bad looking,
is she?"

11
The Shower of Sand

"**I**'m afraid it's not quite the thing to enter people's houses in this fashion," whispered Juve as he and Fandor found themselves in the hall of Doctor Chaleck's little house in the Frochot district.

It was about midnight, and through the fanlight of the outer door a dim twilight enabled the detective and the journalist to get an idea of the place in which they stood. It was a fairly large hall with double doors on both sides, leading into the drawing and dining rooms. At the far end rose a winding staircase, and under it a door leading to the cellar. A hanging lamp, unlit, was suspended from the ceiling. The walls were covered with dark tapestries.

Juve and Fandor remained silent and motionless for several minutes. They had every reason to be uneasy, for their methods were questionable, to say the least, and they knew the doctor was at home. The lodgekeeper of the Cité had seen him return about two hours ago. For a moment Juve had considered ringing in the most natural manner in the world and afterward contriving some explanation. But the silence, the peace that prevailed, and the conviction that Doctor Chaleck, quite off his guard, must be enjoying deep slumber, prompted him to enter the house unannounced. If the door was only bolted, if it was not secured from within by a latch, the detective might be able to find among his pass keys one that would allow him to open it. Juve was, indeed, equipped like the prince of burglars.

Well, the attempt had succeeded. Without trouble or noise, journalist and detective had made their way into the house.

The detective's plan was to make a sudden entry into Chaleck's bedroom and, in the surprise of a sudden awakening, question the doctor and inspect the fingers of his right hand, which, presumably, had left a telltale trace of blood on the register.

Juve had barely entered the room when Fandor switched on the lights. The two men started back in disgust; the room was empty!

Without pausing, Juve cried: "To the study!"

A moment later they found themselves in the room they knew so well from having spent a whole night there, behind the window curtains. Chaleck wasn't there either. Fandor searched the bathroom nearby, careless of the noise he made, then hurried after Juve to the floor below. He was afraid the doctor might already have made his escape.

Juve quickly reassured him that the windows and shutters of the rooms were hermetically closed; the hall door had not been touched.

Suddenly slight sounds from the floor above became audible. A crackling of the boards, the muffled sounds of hasty footsteps, faint rustlings.

"Chaleck knows we are here," whispered Juve.

The two men cocked their pistols and made a rush upstairs. They had left the electric light burning on the floor above, and at first their eyes were dazzled by the sudden brightness, multiplied by the reflection from the glass that lined the octagonal-shaped landing.

Again the noises were heard. Chaleck or someone else was in the study.

Juve disappeared. He soon returned, bumping into Fandor.

"Where are you coming from?" he cried. "I thought you were behind me."

"I was," replied Fandor, "but I left you to take a look in the study."

"But it was I who was in the study!"

Fandor stared in amazement. "Are you losing your senses?"

"I've just come from there myself!"

"Well, we weren't there together, that's certain. Let's try again."

The two proceeded in the dark to the head of the staircase. With their heels they verified the last step. Then Juve said in a low voice, "I will go forward four paces. I am now in the middle of the landing; I lift the curtain, turn and go in."

The steady tick of the little Empire clock on the mantelpiece assured Juve that he was indeed in the study.

"Well, here I am," and he mechanically flung his hat onto the sofa. But he had hardly uttered these words when Fandor's voice, very clear, but some way off, answered: "I am in the study, too."

Juve now switched on the light. Fandor was not there. Rushing back to the landing, he ran headlong into his friend and the two gripped each other in amazement.

"Look here," exclaimed Fandor, "if I'm not mistaken, you turned to the right past the curtain while I went to the left. There may be two separate entrances to the study."

"Let's stick together this time," said Juve. "I want to get to the bottom of this mystery."

As they came out of the darkness of the passage and plunged into the full light of the room, Juve stopped short. His hat was no longer on the sofa.

Fandor went to the mantelpiece, turned, and confronted the detcctive.

"I stopped the clock a few minutes ago, and here it is ticking and keeping exact time! How do you account for that?"

Juve was about to reply when suddenly, with a dry click, the light went out.

At the same moment Fandor gave a startled cry: "Juve! the door is fastened! We are locked in!"

With one bound Juve leaped for the window. But after opening the casement he could see that thick iron shutters, padlocked, made all hope of escape futile. Fandor was ashy pale. Juve staggered as he moved toward him.

"Walled in!" he cried. "We are walled in!"

But the two men were suddenly confronted by a new terror. The floor appeared to be giving way, and as the descent proceeded, they realized that they were in a kind of elevator.

The study, however, did not drop very far. With a slight shock it reached the end of the run and stopped suddenly.

Juve cried with an air of relief: "Well, here we are, and it now remains to find out where we are."

"Juve! did you feel anything?"

"Yes."

"What is it?"

"I don't know."

They had both just experienced a weird sensation, impossible to define. Slight prickings irritated the skin of their hands and faces. At the same time the air seemed heavier and more difficult to breathe, and they heard a soft, vague crackling. With some difficulty Juve turned on his flashlight. By its faint glimmer the two men made a discovery. A fine rain of sand was falling from the ceiling.

"It's collapsed!" cried Fandor.

"We're done for!" replied Juve.

They passed through some awful moments. All around them the sand gathered and rose.

Juve tried to comfort his friend. "It would take an enormous amount of sand to fill this room and bury us alive. It will stop falling soon."

But as the level of the sand rose on the floor, they observed by the flickering gleam of the flashlight that the ceiling was now being lowered little by little.

Fandor raised his arm and touched it. They were about to be crushed.

"Juve, don't let me die this way. Kill me!"

His comrade, at first paralyzed by shock, now felt an unspeakable fury rising in him. He began beating the walls with his fists, shaking the furniture. He seized a chair and drove it against the door. The chair struck some metal with a ring and broke.

Releasing a loud sigh, the detective took out his revolver. He would at least save his friend the torments of an awful death. Suddenly a fearful crash resounded. The moving mass of sand was falling away from them into some gaping hole below. At the same time fresh, moist air reached them and refreshed their lungs.

Juve was bending over to examine what had taken place when the floor suddenly gave way under his feet and he fell, dragging Fandor with him. They found themselves mid-leg in water, but otherwise unhurt.

Juve's voice rang out: "We are saved! I see now what happened! Our trap had a thin flooring, and, when down, it rested on a fragile arch. That arch gave way, and with the sand we have tumbled into the sewer of the place Pigalle, which, if I am not mistaken, connects with the main of the Chaussée d'Autin. Come along, Fandor, we'll find the way out of this before long."

Floundering in the mud, they made their way along the drain until Juve gave a cry of triumph. On the left wall of the vault his hand encountered iron rings one above the other. It was a ladder leading to one of the manholes. He quickly climbed up and, with a vigorous push, raised the heavy slab. In a few minutes both men had emerged and fell exhausted onto the street.

When Fandor recovered his senses he was lying in a large, dimly lit hall. The first sound he heard was Juve's voice arguing hotly and volubly.

"Why, you're nothing but a pack of idiots! We burglars! It's utter rot. I tell you I'm Juve, inspector of public safety!"

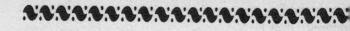

12
Following Josephine

The captives had been recognized, and had been set free. They had barely got a few yards from the police station when Juve took the journalist's arm.

"Hurry!" he cried. "This foolish arrest has made us lose precious hours."

"You have a plan, Juve? What is it?"

"Josephine. We must use her as a bait to catch the others. The girl won't be at Lâriboisière much longer. She will be extremely anxious to leave the place and—"

"And go back to clear herself of treachery in Loupart's eyes? Is that it?" added Fandor.

"Exactly. Accordingly, here is our plan of action. I must go at once to the prefecture and advise Monsieur Havard of our adventure. Meanwhile, you go to the hospital. Find a way to see Josephine, make sure she hasn't left, watch her, and then—wait for me. Within two hours, at the latest, I'll join you."

"All right, Juve, you can count on me. Josephine will not escape."

Fandor was already moving away when Juve called him back.

"Wait! If for one reason or another you need to contact me, telegraph to the Sureté, room forty-four, in my name. I'll see that the messages always reach me."

A quarter of an hour later Fandor was turning into the rue

Ambroise-Paré when he passed a certain woman and gave a start.

"Hullo!" he cried. "That's something we hadn't bargained for," he said to himself.

The woman was walking along the boulevard Chapelle toward the boulevard Barbès. Fandor followed her.

When the great clock of the Lâriboisière struck six, the nurses in the hospital were busy finishing their preparations for the night. The surgeon in Dr. Patel's section was just making his last rounds of patients. With a word of encouragement and cheer he went from bed to bed until he came to the one at the end of the ward. The young woman occupying it was sitting up.

"So you want to leave," exclaimed the surgeon.

"Yes, doctor."

"Then you're not comfortable here?"

"Yes, doctor, but—"

"But what? Are you still afraid?"

"No, no."

The patient spoke these last words so confidently that the surgeon could not help smiling.

"Do you know," he observed, "that in your place I would be much less confident. What are you going to do? Where will you go when you leave here? Come now, you are still very weak; you had better spend the night here. You could go tomorrow morning after the rounds at eleven. It makes much more sense."

The young woman shook her head and replied curtly, "I want to go now, sir. At once."

"All right. They will give you your pass."

The doctor gone, the young woman quickly jumped out of bed and began to dress.

"You don't suppose I'm going to stay here a minute longer than I have to," she grumbled with a laugh to her neighbor, who was watching her enviously.

"Someone waiting for you?"

"Sure there is. Loupart won't be pleased that I'm not back yet."

"Are you going to his place, then?"

"You bet I am."

She said this in a tone that showed plainly that she thought it was the only natural thing to do.

"You were lucky not to have been killed by him. And when he gets hold of you—"

But Josephine laughed happily.

"You don't know what you're saying. Depend on it, if Loupart didn't kill me it's because he didn't want to. He's a crack shot. He must have had his reasons for not wanting me to stay here. I don't know his affairs, and besides, I came here without consulting him."

A vigorous "hush" from the nurse on duty stopped the conversation.

Meanwhile, Josephine finished dressing. A nurse had brought her the clothes she had worn on entering the hospital. She slipped on a faded muslin skirt, laced her bodice, buttoned her boots, and straightened her hair. She was ready.

"I'm off," she cried gaily to the doorman as she held out her pass to him. "Thank God, I'm getting out of here, and I won't be back."

In the street, Josephine walked quickly. She cast a glance at the clock at a cabstand, and found she was behind schedule.

She went along the rue Ambroise-Paré, then turned onto the outer boulevards. Since it was dinnertime, the busy streets of the Chapelle quarter were at their quietest. The bookshops had long since released their employees, and the cafés were closing up to customers. Fandor, having recognized Josephine, followed her closely as she passed the outer boulevards, then the boulevard Barbès.

"Beyond a doubt she is bound for the Goutte-d'Or," he muttered.

A few minutes later, sure enough, she reached her home.

"Very good! The bird is back in the nest. My job is now to watch the visitors who come to call on her."

Opposite Josephine's door there was a bistro. Fandor went in.

"Pen and paper, please," he ordered, planning to drop a line to Juve. He was busy drawing up a detailed map of the neighborhood when, on raising his head, he gave a violent start and, throwing a coin on the table, rushed out of the shop.

"She is well disguised, but there's no mistaking her!"

Without losing sight of the woman he was watching, Fandor reached the Metro station.

"Good Lord! What does this mean?" he wondered. "Where is she off to? She's buying a first-class ticket. Can she have an appointment with Chaleck?" He also bought a ticket and headed for the platform.

"I'm going where she goes," he thought. "But where the devil are we bound for?"

Loupart's mistress was the embodiment of the chic Parisienne. Her gown, tailor-made, was of navy blue, plain but perfectly cut. She wore little shoes with high heels, and no one could have recognized in the well-dressed woman, who got out of the Metro at the Lyons station, the woman who a short while ago had left Lâriboisière.

Josephine had barely taken a few steps on the great Square that divides the boulevard Diderot from the Lyons station when a young man, dressed quietly, came toward her. He looked her over. Then, in a voice of marked cordiality, said, "Can I say a few words to you?"

"But, sir—"

"Two words, mademoiselle. I beg of you."

"Go on," she said at last, after seeming to hesitate.

"Oh, not here; surely you will have a drink?"

The young woman made up her mind.

"Very well, if you like."

The couple headed for a neighboring brasserie, and neither the young man nor Josephine noticed that a passerby had followed them into the place.

Fandor did not take a seat at one of the little tables outside but went inside, cleverly finding a way to observe the two in a glass.

"Is this the person Josephine was to meet?" he wondered. "Can he be a messenger of Loupart's? Yet she did not seem to know him. But what's this?"

Just as the waiter was bringing two glasses of wine to the table where Josephine and her partner sat, the young woman suddenly got up and, without a word, headed for the door.

Fandor walked past the deserted man. He heard the waiter say jokingly, "Not very kind, the little lady, eh?"

"I guess not! Didn't take her long to give me the slip."

Then in a tone of regret the young man added, "Pity, she was a sweet thing."

"That's all right," thought Fandor. "Now I know that Josephine accepted the drink because she thought he was sent by Loupart or one of the gang. As soon as she saw what he was really after, she left in a hurry."

Tracking the young woman, Fandor now felt sure he was going to witness an interesting meeting. Josephine, however, seemed in no hurry. She inspected the illustrated papers in the kiosks and soon reached the box where platform tickets are distributed. Having bought one, she sat down near the foot of the staircase that leads to the snack shops. Behind her Fandor also took a ticket and, going up the stairs, leaned against the balustrade.

"I'm waiting for someone," he said to the waiter who appeared. "You may bring me a cup of coffee."

Within less than five minutes, Fandor saw a shabby-looking man approach Josephine and begin an earnest conversation.

The man took a greasy notebook from his pocket. From it he took a paper that he handed to the young woman, who promptly put it away in her handbag.

Fandor was puzzled. Where was she going? Why had this person given her a ticket?

The man pointed to a train where passengers were already taking their seats.

"The Marseilles train! So Loupart has left Paris!"

Then he called a messenger.

"Go and get me a first-class ticket to Marseilles. Here is the money. Is there a telegraph office nearby?"

"On the arrival platform, sir."

"Right. I will give you a message to take; go and hurry back."

Fandor took out his notebook and scrawled a message:

Juve, Prefecture of Police, Room 44.
Have met Josephine and followed her. She is on the Marseilles train, first class. Don't know her destination. Will wire you as soon as there's anything fresh.

Fandor

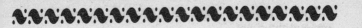

13
Robbery, American Style

"**T**ickets, please."

The guard took the one offered by Fandor.

"Excuse me, sir. There's a problem here," he said.

"This train doesn't go to Marseilles?"

"The train, yes, but this is the last car, bound for Pontarlier. It will be uncoupled at Lyons from this express."

Fandor was nonplussed. All that mattered was that he follow Josephine, ensconced in the compartment next to his.

"Well, I'll get into another car when we start moving; it's so easy with the corridors."

"You can't do that, sir," insisted the guard. "While all the cars for Marseilles in the front of the train are connected, this one is separated from them by a baggage car."

"Then I'll change later, during the night. I have till Dijon, haven't I?"

"You have."

The guard went away. Fandor suddenly asked himself: "Has Josephine made a mistake, too? Or has she a definite purpose in being in a car that is to be uncoupled from the southern express at Dijon to go on toward the Swiss frontier?"

The guard was looking at tickets in Josephine's compartment. Fandor went close enough to listen. He heard the tail

61

end of a conversation between the fair traveler, her companion, and the guard.

"You shall not be disturbed," the guard said, as he withdrew.

When Josephine had boarded the train, Fandor had not dared to watch her too closely, nor the companion she had met on the platform at the last minute. He now decided to take advantage of the corridor to have a look at the man.

He was heavyset and rather common in appearance, despite a prosperous air. A middle-aged man whose jolly face was framed in a beard, giving him the look of an old mariner. Moreover, he was one-eyed.

Josephine was playful, full of smiles and amiability, but she was also somewhat absentminded. The pair certainly had the appearance of being lovers.

Although it was quite early, passengers were already making preparations to spend the night as comfortably as possible. The lamps had been shaded with their little blue curtains, and the doors facing the corridors had been drawn.

Fandor returned to his compartment. Two corners of it were already occupied—the two farthest away from the corridor. One was occupied by a man of about forty with a waxed mustache and the air of an officer in mufti; the other was taken by a young student with a pasty complexion.

The journalist was determined to stay awake, but he had barely settled down when drowsiness crept over him. Rocked by the regular motion of the train he sank into a slumber troubled by nightmares. Suddenly he sprang up. He had the clear impression of someone brushing by him and opening the door to the corridor.

"Who's there?" he murmured in a voice thick with sleep and drowned by the rush of the train. No one answered him. He staggered out into the corridor. At the far end of the carriage a passenger with a long black beard stood smoking a cigar and apparently studying the murky country. Not a sound came from Josephine's compartment. With a shrug of his shoulders and cursing his fears, Fandor returned to his own seat.

Why should he think that, because he was following Josephine, all the passengers in the train were cutthroats and accomplices of Loupart's mistress? Yet five minutes after these sage reflections, Fandor started again. He had distinctly seen, passing along the corridor, two fellows with villainous faces and a suspicious air about them. One of them looked into Fandor's compartment with such a murderous glance that it made the journalist's heart jump.

Fandor glanced at his companions. The officer was sleeping soundly, but the young fellow, though perfectly still, opened his eyes from time to time and cast uneasy glances around him. He pretended to sleep as soon as he caught Fandor watching him.

The train was slowing down; they were entering Laroche station. There was a stop to change engines. The officer suddenly awoke and got out. The compartment with Josephine and her companion was thrown open, and for some reason his neighbor, the student, had moved into it, sitting just opposite the heavyset gentleman.

Fandor, determined to stay awake, abandoned his comfortable seat and settled himself in one of the hammocks in the corridor. He chose the one just opposite Josephine's door. But he was so tired that he quickly fell into a deep sleep. Suddenly a violent shock sent him sprawling to the cross-seat in Josephine's compartment. Dazed, he picked himself up, and a cry of terror escaped him. Three inches from his head was the muzzle of a revolver, held by a big thug wearing a mask.

"Hands up, all of you!" he cried.

Fandor and his companions were too amazed to obey immediately, and the command came again, more forcibly.

"Hands up, and don't move or I'll blow your brains out."

At this point a gnomelike individual, also masked, appeared.

The first one turned to Josephine: "You, woman, out of here!"

Without betraying whether or not she was his accomplice, Josephine hurried out and, slipping between the gnome and the colossus, went to the end of the car, where she cowered.

"Go on!" commanded the thug, who seemed to be the leader. "Go on! Shoot 'em!"

The gnome, with wonderful adroitness, ransacked the coat

and waistcoat pockets of the heavyset gentleman. Trembling with fear, the man offered no resistance. After relieving him of his watch and wallet, they forced him to undo his shirt. Around his waist he wore a broad leather belt.

"Go ahead, Beaumôme. Relieve him of his burden, the fat jackass!"

From the body of the traveler, the stolen belt passed to the big masked robber, who weighed the prize complacently. The belt contained pockets stuffed with gold and bank notes. The two robbers then moved away and toward the other end of the car.

Fandor, furious at being tricked like the simplest of greenhorns, was determined to sound the alarm.

The emergency bell was directly above the pale-faced student. With a bound the journalist sprang for it, but he fell back with a loud cry as he felt a sharp pain in his hand. The student had leaped up and bitten his finger. The pain was so great that Fandor blacked out for a few seconds, and that gave his assailant time to cross the compartment and reach the corridor. At this moment the express slackened its speed and slowly came to a standstill.

"Is it too high to jump?"

Fandor knew the voice. It was Josephine's.

"No," answered someone. "Let yourself go. I'll catch you."

The sound of heavy shoes on the footboard told him that the robbers were getting away. Josephine went with them, so she was their accomplice after all. The journalist ran into the corridor to rush in pursuit. But he recoiled. A shot rang out, broken glass fell around him, and a bullet flattened in the woodwork above his head.

It now seemed to him that the train was gradually gathering speed again. Fandor put his head through the broken glass and searched the darkness outside.

"Ah!" he cried in amazement. There was no longer a train on the track. Instead, the main body of the train was vanishing in the distance, while the car in which he was traveling and the rear baggage car had pulled up. Apparently the robbers had broken the couplings.

At that moment, the heavyset man, having recovered, drew near Fandor and observed the situation.

"Why, we're backing up! We're backing up!" he bellowed with alarm.

"Naturally, we're going down a slope," replied Fandor calmly. The man groaned and wrung his hands.

"My God! The Simplon express is only twelve minutes behind us!"

Fandor now realized that they were in terrible danger. Without delay he made for the car door, ready to jump and risk breaking his bones rather than face the crash that seemed inevitable. But before he could make up his mind to take the leap, a grinding noise became audible. The guard in the baggage car had applied the brakes, and within minutes they had come to a stop.

Fandor and the other traveler rushed frantically out of the car, and two brakemen jumped from the baggage car, crying: "Get away! Save yourselves!"

Clambering over the ties, they jumped a hedge, floundered in a hole full of water, scratching their hands and tearing their clothes. They rolled down a grassy slope, stuck in a plowed field, then fell to the ground, motionless, as a fearful din burst like thunder on the hush of the night. The Simplon express, racing at full speed, had crashed into the two cars left on the rails and smashed them to bits, while the engine and forward cars of the train were telescoped.

14
Night Flight

Loupart just had time to catch Josephine as she jumped from the car when he had to urge his companions to hurry.

"Now, then, boys, let's get moving! Josephine, pick up your skirts and get a move on!"

It was a dark night, with no moonlight, but ideal for the robbers' plans. For a good fifteen minutes the group continued their retreat. From time to time Loupart questioned the "Beard."

"This the way?"

The other nodded. "Keep on going, we'll get there."

Finally they spotted the white ribbon of a road winding up the side of the low hill and vanishing into a small wood in the distance.

"There's the track," declared the Beard.

"To Dijon?"

"No, to Verrez."

"Good. Now stop and listen to me."

Loupart sat down on the grass and addressed them.

"Everything's worked out so far, but we're not finished yet. They took precautions we couldn't foresee. We have only part of the loot. We divvy up tomorrow evening."

He was answered by growls of disappointment.

"I said tomorrow evening," he repeated. "Those who aren't satisfied with that can stop right here. There'll be all the more for the rest of us. Now we'll have to separate. Josephine, you, the Beard, and I will go back together. There's work for us in Paris. You others scatter and take care not to get nabbed; be back in the nest by ten.''

Loupart motioned to the Beard and Josephine to follow him.

''Show us the way, Beard.''

''Where to?''

''The telegraph office.''

''What's up?''

''Why, you idiot,'' replied Loupart, ''we've been robbed! The winedealer's notes are only halves! The swine insured himself for nothing.''

The Beard broke out into recriminations.

''Listen, don't get upset,'' was Loupart's retort. ''Two halves will make a whole.''

''You know where to find the rest?''

''Yes, old man.''

''That's our job tomorrow evening? That's why you're heading for the telegraph office?''

Loupart clenched his fists. ''That and something else; there's bigger game afoot.''

''What?''

''Juve.''

''Damn!'' muttered the Beard, torn between pleasure and fear. ''You've got the beggar?''

''I have.''

''Sure?''

''Sure.''

The little group moved forward in silence. Finally Josephine began to grow tired.

''Say, do we have much farther to go?''

''No,'' replied the Beard. ''Verrez is behind that hill. The main road runs by the row of poplars.''

''All right. Go and wait there with Josephine. I'll catch up with you in a quarter of an hour,'' ordered Loupart. ''I have a wire to send off.''

The others gone, Loupart continued on his way. As a precaution, he took off his jacket, turned it inside out, and put

it on again. The jacket was a trick one: The lining was a
different color, and the pockets were positioned differently.

On reaching Verrez, Loupart turned around. From the top
of the little hill he could see the flames in the distance.

"That's going all right," he thought. "The Simplon express has run into the cars. Things must be a real mess."

Reaching the post office at last, he took up a sheet of paper
and wrote quickly:

> Juve, Inspector of Safety, 142 rue Bonaparte, Paris. All
> is well; found gang complete, including Loupart. Robbery
> committed but failed. Cannot give details. Be at Bercy
> Warehouse alone, but armed, tomorrow at eleven at night,
> near the Kessler House cellars.
>
> Fandor

The clerk held out her hand to take the message. The rogue
was extremely polite.

"Be so good as to pay special attention to this message.
Read it over, madame. Do you understand how important it
is? It must be kept absolutely confidential. I'm counting on
you."

Ten minutes of quick walking brought Loupart once more
to Josephine and the Beard.

"Hullo!" he cried. "Anything new?"

"Nothing."

"Josephine, go down the hill and the first car that comes
along start yelling 'help,' and 'murder.' Got to stop it.
Hurry!"

A few minutes passed. The two men watched Josephine go
down the road and hide in one of the ditches.

"Your heater ready, Beard?"

"Six plugs, Loupart."

"Good! You go to the right; I'll take the left."

Loupart had barely given these orders when a bright gleam
became visible on the horizon, growing larger every minute,
while the noise of a motor broke the silence of the open
country.

Loupart laughed.

"Look, Beard. Acetylene lamps, eh? That car will do the job just fine."

An automobile was getting closer. As it passed by Josephine, she rushed into the road, yelling: "Help! Murder! Have pity! Stop!"

The chauffeur, caught off guard by the sight of a woman appearing so unexpectedly on the lonely road, braked suddenly. Meanwhile, a passenger leaned out of the car.

"What is it? What's the matter?"

As the car was about to stop, Loupart and the Beard rushed out.

"You take the passenger!" cried Loupart. "I'll take care of the chauffeur."

The two thugs sprang onto the footboards.

"No tricks, or I'll shoot! Josephine, truss these birds for me!" cried Loupart.

Josephine took a roll of cord from her lover's pocket and tied the two victims firmly while Loupart gagged them.

"Now, Beard, take them into the field and give them a tap on the head to keep them quiet."

Then he got into the car and skillfully turned it around. When Josephine and the Beard got in, he drove off at full speed with a grim smile.

"And now, Juve, it's between us two!"

15

The Simplon
Express Disaster

The disaster occurred while Loupart and his mates were making off across country. At a curve in the track the Simplon express, traveling at full speed, hit the cars. Lifted by the shock, the engine reared backward on its wheels and fell heavily, dragging with it a baggage car and the first two cars coupled behind it. Then cries of terror rose in the night as the frantic passengers fled from the luxurious train.

Fandor picked himself up and went forward. From the tender a cloud of steam escaped with hoarse whistlings.

The driver held out his two broken arms.

"Give me a hand, for God's sake! Open the tap! There, that hoisted bar. Lift it up. Quick, the boiler is going to burst."

Fandor was still carrying out this maneuver when help began to arrive.

The stoker, less seriously hurt than the driver, had managed to drag himself clear of the wreckage, which was beginning to catch fire. The head guard and the passengers whose seats had been at the rear of the train moved quickly, and the rescue effort began. They searched for the injured and put out the flames.

Those who had fled from the train instinctively followed the road at the foot of the embankment in a frantic stampede, reached Verrez out of breath, and gave the alarm. The countryside was soon in an uproar. A quarter of an hour after the disaster half the neighborhood was up and about. Lights flashed, torches and lamps were being lit everywhere.

"We're just lucky," the conductor said to Fandor, "that the collision happened at the curve where our speed was slackened. Ten minutes sooner and all the cars would have been telescoped." He was still pale with terror.

"Yes, it was luck," replied the journalist as he wiped his face, which was covered with soot and coal dust. "The two telescoped cars were almost empty."

From a neighboring way station the railway officials had telephoned news of the accident. The line was kept clear by telegraph. Word came that a relief train was being sent and would arrive in an hour.

Fandor had quickly regained his composure, and was one of the first to lend a hand in the rescue, turning over the wreckage and freeing the injured. As he passed along the track, he was drawn by the appeals of a man who hurried toward him, wailing: "What a disaster!"

Fandor recognized his fellow passenger as Josephine's lover.

"Yes, and we had a lucky escape. But what has become of your wife?"

In using the word "wife" Fandor was under no illusion; he merely wanted to sound the man out.

"My wife? Ah, sir, that's the terrible part of it. She's not my wife—she's my mistress, and now it's all bound to come out. My wife will hear everything. As for the girl, I don't know what has become of her."

"She knew that you were carrying money?"

"Yes, sir. I am an agent for wines at Bercy, and I was going to pay over dividends to stockholders, one hundred and fifty thousand francs. I recognized one of my men among the robbers, a cooper. He knew that I travel every month, carrying large amounts of money. I am quite sure this robbery was planned beforehand."

"And who are you, sir?"

"Monsieur Martialle, of Kessler & Barriès. Fortunately the money is not lost."

"Not lost! You know where to find the robbers?"

"That I do not, but they have only the halves of the notes. These are worth nothing to them unless they can lay their hands on the corresponding halves. It's a kind of cheap insurance."

"And where are the other halves of the notes?"

"Oh, in a safe place, in the office of the firm at Bercy."

Fandor abruptly left M. Martialle and approached an official.

"When will the line be cleared?"

"In an hour's time, sir."

"There'll be no train for Paris till then?"

"No, sir."

Fandor moved off along the track.

"That's all right, I can make it. I'll have time to send a wire to *The Capital*."

The journalist sat down on the grass, took out his writing pad, and began his article. But he had overrated his strength. He was worn out, body and soul. He had not been writing ten minutes when he fell into a doze. The pencil slipped from his fingers, and he was soon fast asleep.

When Fandor opened his eyes dusk was beginning to gather. It was between five and six o'clock.

"What a fool I've been! I've made a mess of the whole business now," he thought as he ran frantically to the nearest station.

"How soon is the first train to Paris?"

"Two minutes, sir; it is signaled."

"When does it arrive?"

"At ten o'clock."

Fandor threw up his hands.

"I shall be too late. I haven't time to wire Juve and warn him. What an idiot I was to fall asleep like that!"

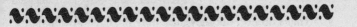

16
A Drama at
the Bercy Warehouse

J uve spent the whole day at the Cité
Frochot. Despite the precautions taken
to keep the failure two days ago a secret, the papers had got
wind of the drama. *The Capital* itself had spoken of it, though
without naming his fellow worker. The staff of the paper was
unaware that Fandor was the other man who had so marvel-
ously escaped from the sewer. Blood-curdling tales were being told about Doctor Chaleck, Juve, Loupart, the house of
the crime, and the affair at the hospital. But to anyone familiar with the actual events, the newspaper accounts were a
far cry from the truth.

And Juve, far from contradicting these misstatements, took
a delight in broadcasting them. It is sometimes useful to give
a false security to the real culprits by allowing the press to
disseminate misleading information.

In the drawing room on the ground floor of Chaleck's
house, Juve first had a long interview with its owner,
M. Nathan, the well-known diamond broker of the rue de
Provence. The poor man was in despair at the thought that
his property had been the scene of the extraordinary events
that were on everybody's tongue. All he knew of Doctor
Chaleck was that that gentleman had been his tenant for four
years and had always paid his rent on time.

"You didn't suspect," asked Juve in conclusion, "the ingenious contrivance of that electric lift in which the doctor installed a study identical to the real one?''

"Certainly not, sir," replied M. Nathan. "Eighteen months ago my tenant asked permission to repair the house at his own expense. As you can imagine, I was glad to comply with his request. It must have been then that the mechanism was built. Do I have your permission to go down to the basement and ascertain its condition?''

"Not before tomorrow, sir, when I will have finished my inspection," replied Juve as he saw M. Nathan out.

The inspector was assisted by detectives Michel and Dupation. They interviewed the old couple in charge of the Cité and various neighbors of Doctor Chaleck, but without finding a clue. Nobody had seen or heard anything.

Toward noon he and Michel, who didn't want to leave the house, decided to send out for a modest lunch. M. Dupation, a fidgety official, used the opportunity to get away.

"Well, gentlemen," he declared, "you are much more up to this business than I, and, besides, my wife expects me for lunch. You don't need any more help from me, do you?''

Juve reassured the superintendent and gave him permission to go. He was only too glad to find himself alone with his lieutenant. The workmen who were repairing the caved-in basement of the house were already gone, and there was no chance of their being back before two o'clock. Thus Juve found himself alone with Michel.

"What I can't understand, sir," said Michel, "is the telephone call we got from here toward morning asking for help at the office in the rue Rochefoucauld. Either the victim herself phoned, and in that case she did not die, as we think, in the early part of the night, or it was not she, and then—''

Juve smiled. "You are right in putting the problem that way, but to my mind it is easy to solve. The call was not made by the murdered woman. Remember, when we raised the body at half-past six it was already cold. Now the call was not made until six, when the woman had been dead some time. That I am sure of, and you will see that the report of the medical expert supports me.''

"Then it was a third person who made it?''

"Yes, someone who wanted to have the crime discovered

as soon as possible and who was counting on the officers coming from the Central Station, but didn't expect Fandor or me to come back.''

"Then you think the murderer knew you were behind the curtain in the study while the crime was being committed.''

"I can't tell about the murderer, but Doctor Chaleck certainly knew we were there. That man must have watched us all night, known the exact instant we left the house, and afterward immediately got someone to telephone or did it himself.''

Michel, becoming more and more convinced by Juve's reasoning, went on: ''At any rate, the existence of two studies, in all respects similar, shows that this was a carefully premeditated plan. But there is something I can't account for. When you came back to the study where we found the dead woman, you found traces of mud by the window brought in by your shoes. You must therefore have been watching through the night the room where the crime was committed.''

Juve was about to put in a word, but Michel, launched on this train of argument, continued: ''Allow me, sir. You are going, no doubt, to tell me that they might during your short absence have carried the body of the victim into the study in question. But I would point out to you that the hair of the poor creature was caked with blood, that some was on the carpet and had even gone through to the flooring beneath. Now if they carried in the body just a little while before we discovered it, that would not have been the case.''

Michel was delighted with his own argument. Juve smiled indulgently.

"My poor Michel,'' he said, ''you would be quite right if I put forward such an explanation. It is certain that the room in which we found the body was that in which the crime took place. It is therefore that in which we were not! As for the marks of mud near the window, they were ours, but transferred from the room in which we were into the room in which we were not! Which again proves that our presence was known to the culprits.

"Furthermore, the candle Doctor Chaleck used to melt the wax to seal his letters had hardly been used. In fact, it only burned a few minutes. Now we found another candle in the same state. So you see that the precautions were well taken, and everything possible was done to lead us astray.

"We see the puppets moving—Loupart, Chaleck, Josephine, others maybe—but we don't see the strings."

"Perhaps the strings that move them are none other than—Fantômas," ventured Michel.

Juve frowned and suddenly fell silent. Then, abruptly changing the conversation, he asked his lieutenant: "You told me, didn't you, that you could no longer appear in the character of the Sapper?"

"That's right, inspector. I was spotted just the day before the crime by Loupart, and so was my colleague, Nonet."

"Speaking of whom," said Juve, "Nonet mentioned vaguely something about an affair at the docks; something that was supposed to have been planned by the Beard and an individual known as the Cooper. Do you know anything about it?"

"Unfortunately no, inspector. I know no more about the matter than you do."

"And what's Nonet up to now?"

"He has left for Chartres."

Juve shrugged his shoulders. He was annoyed. Perhaps if Léon, nicknamed Nonet, had not been transferred he would now have some clues to the dock affair.

After persuading Michel to devise a new disguise that would allow him to mix once more with the Cyphers back at the Comrades' Tryst, Juve went down to the basement to supervise the workmen, who were now back, while Michel busied himself with an inventory of the papers found in Doctor Chaleck's study.

Leaving the house toward half-past seven in the evening, Juve went slowly down to the rue des Martyrs, pondering the events of the past few days. As he reached the boulevards the cries of the paperboys drew his attention. An ominous headline was displayed in the papers the crowd was struggling for: "ANOTHER RAILROAD ACCIDENT. SIMPLON EXPRESS TELESCOPES MARSEILLES LIMITED. MANY VICTIMS."

Juve anxiously bought a paper and scanned the list of the injured, afraid he would find Fandor's name among them. But as he read the details and learned that those in the de-

tached car had escaped, he felt somewhat relieved. Hailing a
taxi, he drove off to the prefecture in search of more precise
information.

"A message for you, M. Juve."

The detective, hurrying home, was passing the porter's
lodge. He pulled up short.

"For me?"

"Yes—it's certainly your name on the telegram."

Juve took the blue envelope with distrust and uneasiness.
He had given his home address to no one. He glanced over
the message and breathed a sigh of relief.

"The dear fellow," he muttered as he went upstairs. "He's
had a narrow escape. But all's well that ends well."

After a quick change of clothes and a bite of dinner, Juve
set off again. He jumped into a train for the boulevard St.-
Germain and got off at the Jardin des Plantes. Then, saun-
tering along, he headed for Bercy by the docks, which were
covered as far as the eye could see with rows and rows of
barrels.

About two hours later Juve, who had been wandering about
the vast labyrinth of wine docks, began to grow impatient. It
was already fifty minutes past the appointed hour, and the
detective was beginning to feel uneasy. Why was Fandor so
late? Something must have happened to him! And then why
had he chosen such a strange meeting place!

Suddenly Juve started. He recalled his talk that afternoon
with Michel and the reference to the affair of the docks in
which the Beard and the Cooper were implicated. What if he
had been lured into a trap!

The detective's reflections were suddenly cut short by unusual and alarming sounds. He thought he heard the shrill
blast of a whistle, followed by the rush of footsteps and a
collision of empty barrels.

Juve held his breath and crouched down under the shed in
which he had been standing. He thought he saw the outline
of a shadow passing slowly in the distance. He was stealthily
following in its tracks when he heard a click.

"Two can play at that game," he growled between his

teeth as he cocked his revolver. The shadow disappeared, but the footsteps went on.

Disguising his voice he called out, "Who goes there?"

A sharp summons answered him, "Halt!"

Juve was about to shout to his mysterious neighbor to do likewise when a shot rang out, followed by another. Juve saw where the shots came from. His assailant was barely fifteen paces away from him, but luckily the shots had gone wide.

"Use up your cartridges, my friend," muttered Juve. "When you get to number six, it will be my turn."

The sixth shot rang out. This was the signal for Juve to spring forward. Leaping over the barrels, he went toward the shadow he had spied at intervals. Suddenly he gave a cry of triumph. He was face to face with a man. His cry soon changed into one of surprise.

"You, Fandor?"

"Juve!"

"So you're shooting at me, now, are you?"

As an answer, the journalist held out his revolver, which was fully loaded.

"But what are you doing here, Juve?" he asked.

"You wired to me to come."

"No, I didn't!"

Juve took the telegram from his pocket and held it out to Fandor, but as the two men drew close together, they were startled by a lightning flash, and a report. A bullet whistled past their ears. Instinctively they lay flat between two barrels, holding their breaths.

Juve whispered instructions: "When I give the signal, fire at anything you see or in the direction of the next shot."

The two men raised their heads slowly and noiselessly.

"Ah," cried Juve as he fired at the rapidly fleeing figure.

"Did you see?" whispered Fandor, clutching Juve's arm. "It's Chaleck."

Juve was about to leap up and start in pursuit when he heard a series of dull thuds, the overturning of barrels, stifled curses, and cracking planks. These noises were followed by the footsteps of a group of men drawing near, by words of command, and shrill whistles.

"What's all that now?" asked Fandor.

"The best thing that could happen for us," replied Juve. "The police are coming. These docks are a refuge for all kinds of tramps and crooks who are rounded up from time to time. That's probably what we're about to see."

Juve had scarcely finished speaking when several shots rang out, followed by a general uproar. Then a great blue flame suddenly rose, died away, and flared up again. Thick smoke permeated the atmosphere.

"The kegs of alcohol have been ignited!" cried Juve.

The two men now had to think of their own safety. Evidently thugs had been tracking them for more than an hour, guided by Doctor Chaleck. But they soon found that their retreat was cut off by a ring of flames.

"Let's head for the Seine," suggested Fandor, who had discovered a break in the ring of fire. There was another explosion. From a burst cask a spurt of liquid fire shot up, closing the circle. It had become impossible to pass through in any direction.

They heard the cries of the rabble, the whistles of the officers. In the distance they could hear the fire engines moaning dolefully. The heat was growing unbearable, and the ring enclosing Fandor and Juve was narrowing. Suddenly Juve pointed to an enormous empty cask that had just rolled beside them.

"Have you ever looped the loop?" he asked. "Hurry up, get in. We'll let it roll down the slope of the dock into the river."

In a few minutes the cask was rolling at top speed. Juve and Fandor guessed by the crackling of the outer planks and by a sudden rise in the temperature that they were passing through the flames. Finally the great vat reached the river, plunging into the waves with a dull thud.

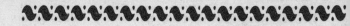

17
On the Slabs
of the Morgue

As he turned at the far side of the Pont St. Louis, Doctor Ardel, the celebrated medical jurist, caught sight of M. Fuselier, the magistrate, chatting with Inspector Juve in front of the morgue.

"I am behind schedule, gentlemen. So sorry to have kept you waiting."

M. Fuselier and Juve crossed the tiny court and entered the semicircular lecture room, where daily lessons in forensic medicine are given to the students and the top men of the detective bureau.

Doctor Ardel, leading his guests, did the honors. "The place is not exactly cheerful. In fact, it has an unpleasant reputation. But anyhow, gentlemen, it is at your disposal. Monsieur Fuselier, you will be able to investigate in peace; Monsieur Juve, you will be at liberty to ask your client any questions you choose."

The doctor spoke in a loud voice, emphasizing each word with a jolly laugh, good-natured, devoid of malice, yet making an unpleasant impression on his two visitors, who were less at home than he was in the gruesome place they had just entered.

"You will excuse me," he went on, "if I leave you for a couple of minutes to change into my overalls and put on my rubber gloves?"

The doctor gone, the two men instinctively felt a need to talk to counteract the grim atmosphere of the morgue, where so many unclaimed corpses, so much human flotsam, had come to sleep under the inquiring eyes of the crowd before being given to the common ditch, being no more than an entry in a register and a date: "Body found so and so, buried so and so."

"Tell me, my dear Juve," asked M. Fuselier. "As soon as I got your message this morning I immediately acceded to your wish and asked Ardel to have us both here this afternoon, but I hardly understand your object. What have we come here for?"

Juve, with both hands in his pockets, was walking up and down in front of the dissecting table. At the Magistrate's question he stopped short, and, turning to M. Fuselier, replied.

"Why have I come here? I hardly know myself. It's everything or nothing. The key to the puzzle. I tell you, Monsieur Fuselier, things are becoming increasingly tragic and baffling."

"How's that?"

"The part played by Josephine is becoming less and less clear. She is Loupart's mistress; she informs against him, is shot by him, and then, according to Fandor, becomes in some manner his accomplice in a robbery so daring that you must search the annals of American criminality to find its like."

"You are referring to the train affair?"

"Yes. Now, leaving Josephine on one side, we are confronted with two enigmas. Doctor Chaleck, a man of the world, a scholar, crops up as leader of a gang of criminals. What we know for certain about him is that he fired at Josephine, that he was involved in the affair of the docks—no more. There remains Loupart; and about him being the real culprit we know nothing. There is no proof that he killed the woman. In order to prove that, we have to know who that woman is and why she was killed, and also how. The how and why of the crime alone might well give us the answer."

"What trail are you following?"

"The dead woman's. The body we are about to examine will show me where to direct my search."

M. Fuselier, looking at the detective with a penetrating eye, asked, "Certainly you don't suspect Fantômas?"

"You are right, Monsieur Fuselier," he replied. "Behind Loupart, behind Chaleck, everywhere and always it is Fantômas I am looking for."

Whatever information the detective was about to impart to the magistrate was cut short by the return of Doctor Ardel.

"We are going to work now, gentlemen," he announced. "I need not remind you, of course, that the body you are about to see, that of the woman found in the Cité Frochot, has already undergone certain changes due to decomposition, which have modified its aspect."

So saying, Dr. Ardel pressed a button and gave an attendant the necessary order. "Please bring the body from room number six."

A few minutes later a folding door in the wall opened and two men pushed a truck into the middle of the hall. On it was the corpse of the unknown woman.

"I now give you the dead woman to identify," declared Doctor Ardel. "My examination has been carried out and my part as expert is over—I am ready to hand in my report."

Fuselier and Juve bent over the slab on which the body had been placed.

"How can we recognize anything in this countenance destroyed by pitch," cried Juve, "these crushed limbs, this shapeless mass?" And, turning to Dr. Ardel, he asked, "Professor, what did you learn from your autopsy?"

"Very little," replied the doctor. "Death was not due to one blow more than another. A general effusion of blood took place everywhere at once."

"Everywhere at once? What do you mean by that?" asked Juve.

"Gentlemen, that is the exact truth. In dissecting this body I was surprised to find that all the blood vessels had burst—the heart, the veins, the arteries, even the lung cells. More than this, the very bones are broken, splintered into numerous little pieces. Finally, both on the limbs and over the whole body I find a general ecchymosis, reaching from the top of the neck to the lower extremities."

"But," objected Juve, who was afraid the professor would

linger over technical details too complex for him, "what does this suggest to you as the cause of death?"

"A strange idea, Monsieur Juve, and one it is not easy for me to define. You might say that the body of this woman had passed under the grinders of a roller! The body is crushed all over, and there is no point where the pressure might be conjectured to have been greatest."

M. Fuselier looked at Juve. "What can we deduce from that?" he asked. "Professor Ardel demonstrates scientifically the same doubts I had. How did the murderer accomplish this? It becomes more and more of a mystery.

"I do not believe," declared the judge, "that there is any more to see here. It is plain, Juve, that this corpse cannot furnish us with any clues for the inquest."

"The corpse, no," cried Juve. "But there is something else." Then, turning to the professor, he asked, "Could we see the clothes this woman was wearing?"

"Of course."

From a bag that an attendant handed him Juve drew out the garments of the dead woman. The shoes were by a good maker, the silk stockings with open-work embroidery, the chemise and the drawers were of fine linen, and the corset was well cut.

"Nothing," he observed. "Not a mark, not even the name of the shop where it was bought."

He examined her petticoat, her bodice, an elegant blouse trimmed with lace, and the velvet collar that had several spots of blood on it. He then drew a small penknife from his pocket and, kneeling on the floor, proceeded to probe the seams. Suddenly he uttered a muffled exclamation.

"Ah! What's this?" From the lining of the bodice he drew out a thin roll of paper, crumpled, stained with blood, unfortunately torn.

Goodness of God in whom I trust—I do not wish to die with this remorse—I do not wish to risk his killing me to destroy this secret—I write this confession, I will tell him it is deposited in a safe place—yes, I was the cause of the death of that hapless actor! Yes, Valgrand paid for the crime Gurn committed. . . . Yes, I sent Valgrand to the

scaffold by making him pass for Gurn—Gurn who killed
Lord Beltham, Gurn, who I sometimes think must be
Fantômas!

Juve read these lines in an agitated voice, and as he came
to the signature he turned pale and was obliged to stop.

"What is the matter?"

"It is signed—'Lady Beltham.' "

In order that Doctor Ardel, understanding nothing of Juve's
agitation, might grasp the import of the paper just discovered, he would have had to recall the appalling tragedy that
had stirred the whole world three years ago. It was a mystery
that remained unsolved to that hour.*

"Lady Beltham!"

Juve, following his train of thought, pondered that he had
accused this same lady of having, to save her lover, Gurn,
the very day the guillotine was erected on the boulevard,
found a way to send in his stead the innocent actor, Valgrand.
And here in connection with this affair of the Cité Frochot
he found Lady Beltham involved in the puzzle whose solution
he was so eager to find.

Juve again read the momentous paper he had just unearthed. "It is plain," he thought, "that the lady, criminal
though she might be, was first and foremost Fantômas's mistress. And this paper he held in his hands was the tail end of
her confession—the remains of a document in which in a fit
of remorse she had confessed the truth."

Taking the cryptic statement line by line, Juve wondered:
"What do these phrases signify? How to extract the whole
truth from these few words? 'I do not want him to kill me in
order to destroy the secret'! When Lady Beltham wrote that,
she was terrified of Gurn. Then again, what did this other
expression mean?—'Gurn who I sometimes think must be
Fantômas.' She did not know, then, the precise identity of
her lover! Oh, the wretch! To what depths had she sunk?"

Then, as he asked himself these questions, Juve shook from
head to foot. Like a thunderclap he thought he saw the truth
he had been following so eagerly. What had become of Lady

*See *Fantômas*.

Beltham? Must he not come to the conclusion that this woman whose face had been crushed out of all recognition by the murderer was none other than the lady? How else explain the discovery in her bodice of the betraying document? Who but she could have had it in her possession? Who else could have so sedulously concealed it?

Juve read over another clause—"I will tell him it is deposited in a safe place"—Feverishly he took up the garments trailing on the ground, carefully examining their fabrics.

"It is impossible," he thought, "that there should not be another document. The beginning of this confession—I must have it!"

Suddenly he stopped searching. "Damn it all!" And he pointed out to M. Fuselier, disguised in the lining of a loose pocket in the petticoat—a fresh hiding place, but torn and empty.

"This woman had split up her confession into several portions. And if she was murdered, it was certainly to strip her of these compromising papers. Well, the murderer attained his object. Look, Fuselier, this empty cache is the proof of what I have said, and chance alone allowed the paper concealed in the collar of this bodice to fall into my hands."

The detective still groped and pondered, hardly hearing the questions the professor and the magistrate were asking him. Finally he got up and, with a distracted gesture, took the arm of M. Fuselier and dragged him before the stone slab on which the corpse, but recently unknown, smiled a ghastly smile.

"Monsieur Fuselier, the dead woman has spoken. This is the body of Lady Beltham!"

"But who, then, is Doctor Chaleck? Who can Loupart be?"

Juve replied without hesitation. "Ask Fantômas the names of his accomplices!"

And leaving him and Doctor Ardel without any farewell Juve rushed from the morgue, his features so distorted that as they passed him people drew aside, amazed and murmuring, "a madman or a murderer!"

18
Fantômas's Victim

"**Y**ou understand my object, Fandor? Until now I have worked un-aided. I wanted to unearth Fantômas and bring him to head-quarters, saying to my superiors, 'For three years you have maintained this man was dead. Well, here he is! I have put the cuffs on the most terrible criminal of modern times.' Well, I must forgo my little triumph. We must now work in the open. Public opinion must come to our aid."

"Then you want me to write my article?"

"Yes, and tell all the details. Wrap it up by putting the question squarely: 'Is Fantômas still alive?' Then sum up the affirmative. Now, be off. I want to read your article this evening in *The Capital*."

Fandor had just left his detective friend when old Jean, the only servant that Juve tolerated in his private quarters, entered the room.

"Don't forget the person who is waiting in the parlor, sir."

"Ah, yes. Someone who comes to see me at home when nobody knows my address should be interesting. Show him in, Jean."

Juve placed his revolver within reach as Jean announced: "Maître Gérin, notary."

Juve rose, motioned his visitor to a chair, and inquired about the object of his visit.

Maître Gérin bowed respectfully. "I must apologize," he

said, "for disturbing you at home, sir. But it concerns a matter of such importance and involves names so terrible that I could not utter them within the walls of the Sûreté. What brings me here is a crime that must be attributed to Fantômas or his followers."

"Speak, sir. I am all attention."

"Monsieur Juve, I believe that one of my clients, a woman, has been killed. For some time I have had a certain sympathy—and I don't disguise it—an immense curiosity concerning her because she was actually involved in the mysterious affairs of Fantômas."

"The name of the woman, counsel, please?"

"The name of the woman who, I fear, has been murdered is—Lady Beltham!"

Juve gave a sigh of relief. It was the name he had hoped to hear.

Maître Gérin continued: "I have been Lady Beltham's lawyer for a long time, but since the Fantômas case ended in the execution of Gurn and the subsequent scandal attached to the name of Lady Beltham, I have not had any further word from that unhappy woman.

"Indirectly, through the papers, which at times alluded to her, I knew that she had been traveling, then, that she was back in Paris, and had gone to live at Neuilly, boulevard Inkermann. But I did not see her again. It is true that her family matters were settled, her husband's estate entirely wound up. In short, she had no reason to appeal to me professionally."

"To be sure."

"Well, a few days ago, I was surprised to find her in my office. Naturally I refrained from asking her any awkward questions."

Juve interrupted, "In heaven's name, sir, how long has it been since Lady Beltham called on you?"

"Nineteen days, sir."

A sigh of relief escaped Juve. He was afraid all his theories regarding the body at the morgue were going to collapse. "Go on, sir," he urged.

"Lady Beltham, on being shown into my private office, appeared to me much the same physically. But she was no longer the great lady—cold, haughty, a trifle disdainful. She seemed crushed under a terrible load, a victim of some awful mental agony. She appealed to my discretion, both professionally and as a man of honor.

"She then said this: 'I am going to write a letter that, if it fell into the hands of a third person, would bring about a great calamity. This letter I shall entrust to you together with my will, which will tell you what to do with it at my death. I will send you a visiting card with a line in my own handwriting every fortnight. If ever this card fails to come, conclude that I am dead, that they have murdered me, and carry that letter where I tell you—avenge me!' "

"Well, what then?" cried Juve, anxiously.

"That is all, Monsieur Juve. I have not seen Lady Beltham again, nor had any news of her. When I called at her residence I was told she was away. I have come to ask you whether you think she has been murdered."

Juve was pacing the room with great strides.

"Maître," he said at last, "your story confirms all I have suspected. Yes, Lady Beltham is dead. She has been murdered. That letter contained her confession and revealed not only her own crimes but those of her accomplices, of her master—of—Fantômas. Fantômas killed her to free himself of a witness to his evil."

"Fantômas. But Fantômas is dead."

"So they say."

"Have you proof of his existence?"

"I am looking for it."

"What are you going to do?"

"First, I am going to learn where and how Lady Beltham was killed. I will see you again, Maître. Read *The Capital* this evening. In it you will find many interesting surprises."

19

The Englishwoman of the Boulevard Inkermann

"**T**o sum up what I have just learned."

Juve was seated at his desk, and those who knew the great detective would certainly have guessed that he was gravely preoccupied. He was trying to extract some useful information from the notary's visit, some clues essential to the investigation he had undertaken, and that he meant to pursue to the end, come what may. The task was fraught with difficulties and even peril. But the triumph would be great if he should succeed in apprehending the "genius of crime," as he had dubbed Fantômas.

"Lady Beltham had gone to visit Gérin. She was an astute woman after all, and knew how to get her own way. There must have been powerful motives urging her to write that confession. What were those motives? Remorse? No. A woman who loves has no remorse. Fear? Probably, but of what?"

Without being aware of it, Juve had just written the name that haunted him in his notebook: Fantômas.

"Why, of course, Fantômas killed Lady Beltham, and killed her in the house of Doctor Chaleck, an accomplice. And Loupart, another accomplice, got his mistress to write to me, and I believed the denunciation. Loupart got us to tail him, led me unawares behind the curtains in the study, and made me witness that Chaleck was innocent. Oh, the ruse was a clever one. Josephine herself, by the two shots she received some days later at Lâriboisière, became a victim. In short, the trap was sprung and broken.''

The detective snatched up his hat, saw carefully to the charges of his pocket revolver, then cried gravely and solemnly: ''It is you and I now, Fantômas!'' With this he left his rooms.

Juve and Fandor got into a taxicab.

''To Neuilly Church,'' cried Juve to the driver. ''And, now, my dear Fandor, I know I must seem crazy to you. Less than two hours ago I sent you off to write an article, and here I come taking you from your paper and carrying you away in this headlong fashion. But just listen to the tale of this morning's events.''

Juve then gave a full account of Maître Gérin's visit and wound up by saying, ''It is through Lady Beltham that we must unearth that monster, Fantômas.''

''That's all very well,'' replied Fandor, ''but as the lady is dead, how are we going to go about it?''

''By reconstructing the last hours of her life. We are now on our way to Lady Beltham's residence, boulevard Inkermann.''

''And what are we to do when we arrive there?''

''I'll examine the house, which is probably empty, and you'll pump the neighbors, ask questions of the tradespeople. It would attract too much attention if I were to do this myself, and that is why I dragged you away from your work.''

A few minutes later, the taxi pulled up at the corner of boulevard Inkermann.

''The house is number—'' said Juve as he took Fandor by the arm. ''Good heavens, you remember the house! It is the one in which I arrested Gurn three years ago, that day he came to see Lady Beltham, disguised as a beggar.''

The two friends soon found themselves at their destination. Through the garden railing, which was completely covered with a dense growth of ivy, they saw the house, which now looked very dilapidated.

''It looks as if it hasn't been inhabited for a long time,'' said Fandor.

"That's what we want to find out. Go and make your inquiries."

Fandor left his companion and made his way back to the commercial section of Neuilly. He stopped opposite a sign that read: "GARDENING DONE."

"Anyone here?" he called.

An old woman standing in the doorway came forward. "What can I do for you, sir?"

"If I am not mistaken, it was you who attended to Lady Beltham's garden?"

"Yes, sir. We kept her garden in order. But my husband hasn't worked there for several months, as Lady Beltham has been away."

"I heard she was coming back to Paris and called today, but I found the house closed up."

"Oh, I am sorry to hear that. Lady Beltham's an excellent customer and Madame Raymond also bought flowers from us."

"Madame Raymond. She is a friend of Lady Beltham?"

"Her companion. It is now close to a year since Madame Raymond has been living with her. Oh, she's a very pleasant lady; a pretty brunette, very elegant, and not at all proud."

Fandor thought it well not to seem surprised.

"Oh, yes, of course," he cried. "Madame Raymond. I remember now. Lady Beltham's life is so sad and lonely."

"True enough," the woman replied and, lowering her voice: "And then, what with all these tales of noises and ghosts, the house can't be too pleasant to live in, eh?"

Fandor pretended to be well informed. "People still talk of those incidents?"

"Oh, yes, sir."

Fandor did not press the matter, and, taking leave of the woman, he made his way back to the boulevard. As soon as Juve caught sight of him in the distance he ran up eagerly.

"Well?"

"Well, Juve, what have you found out during my absence?"

"In the first place, that it has been exactly sixty-four days since Lady Beltham left Neuilly. I discovered this by examining the dates on a lot of circulars in the mail box. I al-

so had a talk with a butcher's man and learned that Lady
Beltham had a companion.''

''I was bringing you that same news!''

''This Madame Raymond is young, dark, and very pretty.
Can't you guess who she is?''

Fandor stared at Juve.

''You mean—''

''Josephine. It's perfectly clear. We know Lady Beltham
wrote a confession, that Fantômas suspected this and murdered her to get hold of it, and further that Loupart was
involved in this murder. Josephine was introduced to Lady
Beltham by Fantômas. A spy going there to betray the great
lady and possibly entice her later to the Cité Frochot. Let's
hurry. We thought we had to follow the trail of Loupart and
Chaleck, but it's Josephine we mustn't lose sight of. She may
be the key to getting at the truth.''

20
The Arrest of Josephine

Josephine had visitors in her little apartment. There was to be a quiet lunch. On the sideboard attractive dishes were ready, an aroma of onions came from the dark corner in which Loupart's pretty mistress was hastily cooking over the gas.

The somewhat grim faces of Mme. Guinon, Julie, and the Flirt lit up suddenly. Bonzille, the tramp set free by the police the day after the raid in the rue de la Charbonnière, had opened the bottle of vermouth, and Josephine bustled around finding glasses to put on the table.

"Neat or with water?" asked Bonzille, performing his office of cup bearer with comical dignity.

Mme. Guinon asked for plenty of water. Julie shrugged her shoulders indifferently. She didn't care as long as there was drink, while the Flirt, in her cracked voice, breathed in the loafer's ear: "How about a sip of brandy to put with it?"

The drink loosened tongues: they began to cackle. From a drawer Josephine got out a pack of cards, which the Flirt promptly seized, while Julie, leaning familiarly on her shoulder, counseled her: "Cut with the left and watch what you re doing; we shall see if there's any luck for us in the pack."

Josephine had now been back for three days from her painful journey, and she had not yet seen Loupart. The latter, after having abandoned the car in some deserted area, had van-

93

ished with the Beard, instructing his mistress to go home a
if nothing had happened and wait for news of him.

The Simplon Express affair had caused a great stir in the
fashionable world and had produced considerable uneasiness
among the criminal class. No name had been mentioned, and
apparently the police had no definite clues. Still, in the Cha
pelle quarter, and especially in the Goutte-d'Or and the rue
de Chartres, it was noticed that the absence of the chief mem
bers of the Cyphers coincided with the date of the tragedy.

At first there was a slight aloofness toward Josephine or
her return. She was greeted with dubious allusions, equivocal
compliments, and amazement at not seeing Loupart reappear
with her. Josephine told herself that she must at all costs
ingratiate herself with her neighbors. That is why she had
decided to give a luncheon party for her most intimate friends,
who might also be her most formidable opponents. The Flirt,
Julie, even big Ernestine, could not fail to be jealous of the
mistress of a distinguished leader. Besides, she was the pret
tiest woman in the quarter.

Joining the conversation from time to time Josephine
smiled, regaining her confidence. Her plan promised to be a
success.

As they sat down to table the door opened and Mother
Toulouche came in carrying a capacious basket.

"Well," cried the old fence, "I got wind that something
was going on here, and I said to myself, 'Why shouldn'
Mother Toulouche be in it as well?' One more or less don'
matter, eh, Josephine?"

Josephine nodded and made room for her. Before sitting
down the old woman put her basket on the floor.

"If I invite myself, Fifine, I bring something to the feast.
Here are some snails to help out."

Suddenly Josephine, who, despite the general gaiety, was
pensive and preoccupied, got up and ran to the door, an
swering a knock. She was really feeling uneasy about hearing
nothing of her lover. She began to fear that for once the
police might have got the upper hand. It was little Paulot,
the porter's son, who rushed in out of breath.

"Madame Josephine, Mother told me to come up and warn

you that two strange gentlemen were asking for you in the lodge just now."

"Do you know them, Paulot?"

"I don't, Madame Josephine."

"What did they want of me?"

"They didn't say."

"What did your mother say to them?"

"I don't know. I think she told 'em you were in your den."

This information cast a chill over the company. Little Paulot was given a big glass of wine, and when he had left the Flirt observed gravely, "It's the cops."

"What could they want with me?"

Julie tried to console her.

"Anyhow, they won't come up to your place."

Josephine was very upset. Were they after her or Loupart? Why had they left? Would they come back?

In a flash she burst out, beating her fist on the table: "I've had enough of this, not knowing what's going to happen from one moment to the next. Rather than stay here, I'll go and find out."

With a spiteful smile the Flirt suggested, "Go ahead, my girl, they won't be far away. Go and ask them what they want."

"Very well," cried Josephine, "I will."

And the young girl emptied her glass to give her courage.

"And if you don't come back, we'll clean up your room," cried the Flirt after her. "Good luck. Try not to end up in the jug."

Josephine rushed downstairs, and then, after a moment's hesitation, turned and went down the rue de Chartres. At first she noticed nothing unusual or suspicious. The faces of those she met were mostly familiar to her. But suddenly her heart stopped beating. Two men accosted her simultaneously, one on her right, the other on her left.

The one on the right asked very softly, "Are you Josephine Ramot?"

"Yes."

"You must come with us."

"All right," said Josephine, resigned.

A few minutes later Josephine, seated in a cab between the

two men, was crossing Paris. The detectives had given the address: boulevard du Palais.

Loupart's mistress, taken on her arrival to the anteroom adjoining the private rooms of the examining magistrates, had little time for reflection.

To be sure, she was not guilty. Not guilty? Well, at bottom the affair of the Marseilles train made Josephine uneasy. And the story of the car, too, which had been taken by force from unknown travelers. What did the police know about this? When questioned, was she to confess or deny?

A little old man, bald and fussy, appeared at the end of the passage and called her.

"Josephine Ramot, the private room of Justice Fuselier."

Mechanically she went forward between her two captors, who pushed her into a well-lit room, in the corner of which stood a big desk. A well-dressed gentleman was sitting there writing. Opposite him, in the shadow, someone stood motionless. The magistrate raised his head; his face was cold and contained, but not spiteful.

"What is your name?"

"Josephine Ramot."

"Where were you born?"

"Rue de Belleville."

"What is your age?"

"Twenty-two."

"You live by prostitution?"

Josephine blushed and, with an angry voice, cried: "No, your honor, I have a calling. I am a polisher."

"Are you working now?"

Josephine felt awkward.

"Well, to tell the truth, at the moment I have no work, but they know me at Monsieur Monthier's, rue de Malte. It was there that I was apprenticed, and—"

"And since you became the mistress of Loupart, known as the Square, you have ceased to practice an honest calling?"

"I won't deny being Loupart's mistress, but as for prostitution—"

The man Josephine had noticed standing in the shadow

came forward and murmured a few words in the magistrate's ear.

"Monsieur Juve," cried Josephine, moving toward the inspector with her hand out. She stopped short as the detective motioned to her that such a familiarity was not allowed, and the examination was resumed.

The magistrate, having solicited the salient points of Josephine's life, and clearly mapped out the fall of the honest working girl to the status of thief's mistress, and in all probability, accomplice, began the interrogation on the main point.

Finally he narrated the various incidents of the evening begun in the railway that ended with the disaster to the Simplon express. Fuselier reconstructed for Josephine her headlong exit from Lâriboisière, her quick passage through Paris when she was barely convalescent and still suffering from the effects of the fever, her departure in the Marseilles express, where she met the gangsters headed by her redoubtable lover; then the waiting in the silence of the night, the attack, the threats, and finally, after breaking the couplings to the train, the gang's dangerous flight, the headlong rush through the countryside.

The magistrate concluded: "You came to town afterward, Josephine Ramot, in the company of Loupart, called the Square, and his factotum, known as the Beard."

Josephine, embarrassed by the magistrate's steady glance, tried to keep her face expressionless, but as the points of the adventure she had shared grew more definite, she felt herself constantly changing color, and at certain moments her eyelids quivered over her downcast eyes.

He was obviously well informed. That young man who got into the same compartment as M. Martialle must have been with the police. But for that, the judge would never have known precisely what took place. This was definitely a bad beginning.

Josephine now dreaded to see the door open and Loupart appear, handcuffed, followed by the Beard, similarly detained, for she was sure the two men had been nabbed. Hunched up, her nerves tense, Josephine kept her mind fixed on one point. She was waiting anxiously for the first chance to protest.

The magistrate declared: "You three—Loupart, the Beard, and yourself—shared among you the proceeds of the robberies committed."

As soon as she could get a word in, Josephine shouted her innocence. She had not touched a cent from the business. She did not even know what was involved.

The truth was that she was lying sick in the hospital when she suddenly remembered that Loupart had told her to be at the Lyons station, at all costs, on a certain Saturday evening at exactly seven o'clock. Now that particular Saturday was the day after the attempt on her life. As she was much better, she set off in obedience to her lover. She knew no more; she had done no more; she would not have them accuse her of any more.

The young woman grew excited, her voice rose and vibrated. The judge let her have her say, and when she had finished there was silence.

M. Fuselier slowly dipped a pen into the ink, and in his level voice declared, casting a glance in Juve's direction: "After all, what seems clearly established is complicity."

Josephine started—she knew the terrible significance of the term. Complicity meant joint guilt.

But Juve intervened. "Excuse me, in place of 'complicity' perhaps we had better say 'compulsion.' "

"I don't follow you, Juve."

"We must bear in mind, your honor, that this girl is to be pardoned to a certain extent for having obeyed her lover's order, especially at a time when he had gained quite a victory over the police. For in spite of the protection of our people, his attempt against her partially succeeded."

Taken aback, M. Fuselier looked from the detective to the young woman whom he regarded as guilty. Juve's outburst seemed out of place.

"Your pardon, Juve, but your reasoning seems somewhat specious. However, I will not press this charge against the girl; we have something better."

Turning to Loupart's mistress, the judge asked, "What has become of Lady Beltham?"

The question took Josephine by surprise. She turned inquiring eyes toward Juve, who quickly said, "Monsieur Fuselier, this is not the moment—"

The magistrate, dropping this line, again tackled Josephine on her relations with Loupart.

In a flash Josephine made up her mind. She would simulate innocence at all costs. With the craft of a consummate actress, she began in a low voice, which gradually rose and became impressive, insinuating: "How pitiful it is to think that everyone bears a grudge against a poor girl who, one day in springtime, gave herself the pleasure of a lover! Is there any harm in giving oneself to the man who loves you? Who forbids it? No one but the priests, and they have been kicked out of doors!"

The magistrate could not help smiling, and even Juve seemed amused.

"But I am honest, and when I understood what was going on, I wrote to Monsieur Juve. And what thanks did I get? Two bullet holes in my skin!"

M. Fuselier hesitated to turn his summons into a sentence.

21
At the Montmartre Fête

The fête of Montmartre was at its height. In the place Blanche a joyous crowd had gathered around a booth of huge dimensions, splendidly lighted. On the stage a barker, decked out in his own peculiar finery, was delivering his patter:

"Walk in, ladies and gentlemen; only ten centimes! The management of the theater will present to you, without delay, the prettiest woman in the world and also the fattest, who weighs a trifle over six hundred pounds and possibly more, as no scale has yet been found strong enough to weigh her without breaking into a thousand pieces.

"You will also have the rare and exotic sight of a Negro from Abyssinia whose splendid ebony hide has been tattooed in white. Furthermore, a young girl of scarcely fourteen summers will astound you by entering the cage of the ferocious beasts, whose terrible roar can be heard this very moment! And after these incomparable attractions, you will applaud our new full-color cinema—the latest exploit of modern science—showing the recent tour of the president of the republic, and himself in person delivering his speech to an audience as numerous as it is select. You will also see, reproduced in the most stirring and lifelike manner, all the details of the mysterious murder that at this moment engages public interest and keeps the police on tenterhooks. The crime at the Cité Frochot, with the murdered woman, the Empire clock, and

the extinguished candle: all the accessories in full, including
the collapse of the elevator into the sewer. Hurry! Hurry! The
show is about to begin! It has begun!''

Among the throng gathered around the mountebank were
three people who seemed especially amused. They were two
gentlemen, very elegant and distinguished, in evening clothes,
and a pretty woman wearing a loose silk cloak over a low-
cut dress.

She put her lips to the ear of the older of her companions,
who, with his turned-up mustache and gray hair, looked like
a cavalry officer, and murmured: "Look at the guy on the
left, the one passing before the clock seller's booth. He's one
of the gang. He was in the Simplon affair."

The pretty Parisian, so smartly dressed, was none other
than Josephine. The young man with the fair beard was
Fandor, and the cavalry officer was Juve. The three now
worked together. The partnership dated from the afternoon
that Josephine escaped arrest, thanks to Juve's intervention.
He had little belief in the young woman's innocence, but by
getting her on his side he hoped to get to Loupart.

Juve was talking to a ragged Arab selling nougat to passersby.

"Aye, sir," explained the Arab. "I have been tailing little
Mimile since two this afternoon."

"Bravo, Michel. Your disguise is a complete success."

Josephine suddenly came close and, pulling Juve by the
sleeve, pointed to a group of people who were crossing the
place Blanche. Leaving the Arab, Juve began to follow this
group at once, motioning to Josephine and Fandor to stay
close behind. The three threaded their way through the crowd
with a thousand precautions, trying to avoid attracting attention, yet not losing sight of their quarry. All three had recognized Loupart!

The outlaw, dressed in a long peasant blouse, with a tall
cap, and armed with a club, was walking among a half-dozen
individuals similarly attired. By their clothing they would be
taken for cattle herders from La Villette.

The group proceeded slowly in the direction of the place
Pigalle, and Juve, who was pressing hard on his quarry,
slowed his pace in order to put a little distance between them.

The square, which was surrounded by brilliantly lit restaurants, was a flood of light, and the detective did not want to draw any attention to himself. Moreover, the pseudo cattle drivers had stopped, too. Gathering around Loupart, they listened attentively to his remarks, delivered in hushed tones. They were obviously accomplices of the robber, who, perhaps, realized that they were being followed.

Fandor, who had put his arm through Josephine's, felt the young woman's heart beating as though it would burst. They were all playing for high stakes. Josephine, especially, was in a compromising and dangerous position. She ran the risk of being spotted by one of the many satellites of the Cyphers, in which case she would be doomed.

Fandor encouraged her with a few kind words.

"You know, mademoiselle, you mustn't be frightened. If I am not mistaken, Loupart is about to be nabbed, and once he is in Juve's hands he won't get out of them in a hurry."

This did not seem to do much to ease her nerves, and Fandor, a bit skeptical, asked himself whether in reality the girl was on their side or just playing another game.

At this moment Loupart, separating himself from his companions, entered a restaurant that had the words THE CROCODILE inscribed on its front in dazzling letters. The Crocodile was made up of a large hall on the ground floor and a dining room on the first floor reached by a little stairway and guarded by a giant clad in magnificent livery. Above this were apartments and private rooms.

As it was near midnight, a number of carriages were bringing couples in evening dress who mounted the staircase. To their great surprise, Fandor and Josephine saw Loupart head for this staircase. The cattle driver's long smock would certainly make an odd impression here. What was the robber's game now? Juve gave hasty directions.

"It's all right. I know the house. It has only one exit. You, Ramot," he went on, addressing the young woman, "go up to the first floor and take your place at a table. Here's some money, order champagne and don't be too stiff with the company."

Josephine nodded and went upstairs.

Juve and Fandor followed a few minutes later and took up

a strategic position at a table near the doorway. Fandor had a view of the room, and Juve commanded the hall and stairway. From the room came a confused hum of laughter, cries, and dubious jokes. A Negro, dressed in red and armed with a gong, capered among the tables, dancing and singing.

Fandor caught sight of Josephine, who appeared to be carrying out Juve's instructions. Beside her was a giant of a man with a red complexion and a clean-shaven face, whose Anglo-Saxon origin was beyond doubt. Fandor knew the face; he had seen the man somewhere. He remembered his square shoulders and bull-like neck, and the enormous biceps that strained through his shirtsleeves.

"Why it's Dixon," he cried suddenly, "the American heavyweight champion!"

Juve signaled to the waiter to bring him the bill as he fitted a monocle into his right eye.

Fandor stared at him, surprised. "Well, Juve, when you set yourself up as a man of the world, you omit no detail."

Juve made no reply for a few moments. Then he turned to his companion. "Who else do you see in the room?"

Fandor looked carefully, and then made a gesture of amazement.

"Chaleck! Chaleck is over there eating his supper!"

"Yes," said Juve simply, "and you are stupid not to have seen him before."

The profile of the mysterious doctor was in fact outlined very sharply at a table, amply served and covered with bottles and flowers, around which a group of people—men and women—had taken their places.

Without turning his head Juve remarked, "Judging by the action of the person who is at this moment lighting a cigar, the supper is almost over."

"Come now, Juve, do you have eyes in your back? How can you know what's going on at Doctor Chaleck's table while you're looking in the opposite direction?"

Juve handed his eyeglass to the journalist.

"Ah! Now I see! A trick eyeglass, with a mirror in it—not a bad idea."

"It's very simple," murmured Juve. "The main thing is to have thought of it. Come on, let's go down."

"What? And desert the doctor?"

"An arrest should never be made in a public place if it can be avoided. Here, give me your card so I can send it up with mine."

Juve called M. Dominique, the manager and, pointing out Chaleck to him, said, "Monsieur Dominique, please give our cards to that gentleman and say that we are waiting outside to speak to him."

In a few moments Chaleck came out of the hall to the place Pigalle. His face was calm and his expression unmoved. Juve laid his hand upon the doctor's shoulder and, signaling to a subordinate in uniform, cried: "Doctor Chaleck, I arrest you in the name of the law."

Chaleck quietly flicked off his cigar ash and smiled. "Do you know, Monsieur Juve, I am not pleased with you. I read in the papers, during a recent holiday abroad, that you had pulled my house absolutely to pieces! That was not nice of you, when we had been on such good terms."

This speech was so startling, so totally unexpected that Juve, though not easily shaken, found himself at a loss for words.

Meanwhile, Chaleck quietly allowed himself to be dragged toward the station in the rue Rochefoucauld.

"The fellow," thought Juve, "must have got his whole case prepared—he'll give us a run for our money. Still it must—"

The detective gave a loud yell. They had just got to the point where the rue Rochefoucauld is intersected by the rue Notre-Dame de Lorette: a cab drawn by a big horse was moving in one direction, and a bus was coming from another. It had already cleared the rue Pigalle, and in a second would cut across the rue Rochefoucauld, when Chaleck, literally coming out of the Inverness coat he wore, leaped ahead of Juve, dodged under the cab and boarded the bus, which quickly drove off. All this had been accomplished in an instant.

Left dumbfounded, face to face, Juve and Fandor, together with the officer, looked at the only token Chaleck had left: an elegant Inverness cloak with capes, which, oddly enough, had shoulders and arms—arms made of India rubber. It was

such a good imitation that through the cloth the arms gave
the distinct impression of being human arms.

Juve cursed their bad luck, then turned to Fandor and cried,
"How about Loupart?"

The two men hastily returned to the rue Pigalle. They had
expected to stand on guard before The Crocodile again. But
as they reached the square Juve and Fandor discovered that
there were more surprises in store for them. A powerful car
was slowly driving away. In it was the American, Dixon,
with Josephine beside him.

Was the girl using them? That was the most important
thing to find out.

The car drove off at a good pace toward the place de Cli-
chy. A minute later, Juve was bowling after them in a taxi,
calling to Fandor as he left: "Look after the other."

Fandor understood that "the other" referred to Loupart,
and carefully pumped M. Dominique. But he could get no
further information from him, so, after waiting an hour for
Juve to return, he went home to bed feeling far from easy in
his mind.

Juve followed the American through Billancourt, past Sèvres
Bridge, and finally into the Bellevue district, when, opposite
Brimboison Park, Dixon, with the air of a proprietor, took
his car into a fine-looking estate. Then, having housed the
car, the boxer, with Loupart's mistress, went into the house,
which remained lit up for about half an hour. Then everything was plunged again into darkness.

Juve had left his taxi at the bottom of the hill and, having
cleared the low wall of the grounds, hid himself in view of
the house. He waited until daybreak, but nothing happened
to disturb the peace and hush of the night. And then, unwilling to be seen in his evening clothes by chance passersby,
he regretfully returned to the rue Bonaparte.

22
The Boxer's Whim

An old servant had brought out morning coffee to the arbor in the garden. It was about eight o'clock, and in the shady retreat the freshness of springtime reigned. Soon the well-built figure of Dixon, dressed in white flannels, could be seen coming down the gravel walk. He bent under the arch of greenery that led to the arbor and seemed vexed to find it empty. Obviously the boxer wasn't planning to have breakfast alone, and, to while away the time until his companion appeared, he lit a cigarette.

Suddenly the door of the house opened and Josephine—a gracious apparition wrapped in a kimono of bright silk and smiling at the fine morning—slowly walked down the steps and stopped, blushing. Someone came to meet her—it was Dixon.

The big man, too, seemed moved. Lowering his eyes, he asked, "How are you this morning, fair lady?"

"And you, Monsieur Dixon?"

"Mademoiselle Finette, the coffee is served. Won't you join me?"

The two young people broke their fast in silence, exchanging only monosyllables—to ask for a napkin, a plate, the sugar. At last, overcoming his bashfulness, Dixon said in a voice full of entreaty, "Will you always be so hard-hearted?"

Josephine, embarrassed, evaded the question, and with a

show of gaiety to hide her confusion, remarked, "This is an awfully nice place you've got here."

The boxer answered her by describing the calm and simple delights of a country life in springtime. Slipping his arm around her supple waist, he asked softly: "As you consented to come this far with me, why did you put me off afterward? Why resist me so stubbornly?"

"I was a little drunk yesterday," she said. "I don't know what I did or why I came here with you." And then, with a touch of sadness, "Naturally, finding me in such a place you took me for a—"

"Sure enough," replied the American. "But I can see you are not like the others."

"And what attracts me to you," continued Josephine, "is that you are not a brute. Why, yesterday evening—if you had wanted—when we were alone together, eh?"

And she gave Dixon such a queer look that he asked himself whether she did not think he was a fool for having respected her.

"I like you very much," he said, "more than any other woman. In a month I'll be going back to America. I already have a great deal of money, and I'll earn much more there. If you come with me, we'll never be separated again. What do you think?"

Josephine was at first amused by his offer but she gradually began to take it more seriously. She would see the world, be elegant, rich, well dressed. Her future would be secure, and there would be no more trouble with the police. But, on the other hand, it might become terribly boring after the exciting life she had led. And there was Loupart. It was true that he sometimes mistreated her, but he had only to come back and speak to her and she would again be submissive, loving, and tractable. And, strangely, there was also—just lately—at the bottom of Josephine's heart a feeling of friendship, almost affection, for the stern and thoroughgoing detective, Juve, to whom she owed her escape from a very bad fix. Fandor, too, she liked pretty well. She valued the daring journalist, quick, full of courage, and yet a good sort, free from prejudice. The more she thought about it, the more Josephine felt herself to be strikingly complex. She felt that she could not analyze her feelings, she was incomprehensible even to herself.

"Let me think it over a little longer," she said. Dixon rose ceremoniously.

"Dear friend," he declared, "you are at home here as long as you care to stay, and I hope you will consent to have lunch with me at one o'clock. From now till then I leave you alone to think at your leisure."

The old servant had gone shopping, so Josephine had the place to herself. After exploring the charming villa from top to bottom she strolled delightedly amid the lovely scenery of the park. As she was about to turn into a narrow path, she uttered a loud cry. Loupart stood before her. The leader of the Cyphers had his evil look and savage smile.

"Pleased to meet you!" he cried, then asked sardonically: "Which would Madame prefer, the pigsticker or the heater?"

Terrified, Josephine stepped backward until she rested against the trunk of a great tree. Loupart carelessly took out his revolver and his knife: He seemed to be uncertain which weapon to use.

"Loupart," stammered Josephine in a choking voice, "don't kill me—what have I done?"

The thief snarled. "Not only do you squeal to Juve, but you let yourself be carried off by the first man that comes along. You don't think twice about making a fool of me."

Josephine fell on her knees in the thick grass. Suddenly a wave of remorse swept over her. She was overcome at the thought that she could have endangered her lover even for a moment, that she could have informed the police. She was honestly maddened by the thought that Loupart had almost been arrested, thanks to her. Yes, he was right; she deserved to be punished. But as for having wronged him, that wasn't true. She protested with all her might against his accusation of unfaithfulness.

"I was wrong to listen to Dixon, to come here, but in spite of appearances—Loupart, believe me, I've been faithful to you."

Loupart shrugged his shoulders. "Well, we'll leave that for the moment. Right now you're going to do what I tell you without a word of protest."

Josephine's heart stopped; she knew this preamble. She tried to turn the conversation.

"And how did you get here?"

"How did you get here yourself?"

"Monsieur Dixon's car."

"And who followed you?"

"Why—no one."

"No one?" jeered Loupart. "Then what was Juve doing in the taxi that was following you?"

Josephine uttered an exclamation of surprise. Loupart went on, satisfied with himself. "And what was I up to? I was cozily hidden on the springs behind the taxi the worthy inspector was riding in."

Loupart was teasing, and that showed he was in good humor again. Josephine put her arms around his neck and hugged him.

"It's you I love, and you alone—let's go, take me away, won't you?"

Loupart freed himself from the embrace.

"Since you're at home here—the American said as much— I might as well profit by it. You stay here until this evening. At five you will be at the markets, and so shall I. You won't recognize me, but I'll speak to you, and then you'll tell me exactly where this boxer keeps his loot. I want a full plan of the house, a set of keys, all the usual stuff. Tonight I've got something new for Juve and his crew, and you'll have a part to play, too."

Josephine, panting, didn't take in this last sentence. She flushed crimson, perspiration broke out on her forehead, a great agony tightened her heart. She, so docile till then, so devoted, suddenly felt an immense qualm, an awful shame at the thought of being guilty of what her lover demanded. Against any other man, she would have obeyed, but to act this way toward Dixon, who had treated her so considerately, she felt was beyond her powers. Here Josephine showed herself truly a woman. While she was determined not to betray Loupart, she would not destroy the boxer's memory of her. She hesitated to betray him and unwittingly proved the truth of the philosopher's dictum: "The most honest of women, though unwilling to encourage, are never sorry to leave behind a little regret!''

But Loupart wasn't going to stay there discussing such subtleties with his mistress. He never gave his orders twice. To seal the reconciliation he planted a hasty kiss on Josephine's cheek and vanished. A crackling sound marked his passage through the thickets. Josephine was once more alone in the great park around the villa.

Fandor and Dixon were having tea in the drawing room. The journalist had come, he said, to interview Dixon about his fight with Joe Sans, the Negro champion of the Sudan, which was to take place the next day. After getting various details on weight, diet, and other trifles, Fandor inquired with a smile: ''But to keep in good form, Dixon, you must be as sober as a camel, as chaste as a monk, eh?''

The American smiled. Fandor had told him a few moments before that he had seen him supping at The Crocodile with a pretty woman. He meant to find out what the relations were between the boxer and the girl.

The allusion to that evening loosened the American's tongue. Absorbed by the pleasing impression his pretty partner had made on him, Dixon began talking on the subject. He belonged to that class of men who, when they are in love, want the whole world to know it.

The American had put the young woman on such a pedestal of innocence and purity that Fandor couldn't help wondering if he was being ridiculed. But Dixon did not conceal his intention to elope with Josephine and take her to America. Suddenly he got up.

''Come on,'' he said. ''I'll introduce you to her.''

Fandor was about to protest, but the American was already scouring the house and searching the park, calling: ''Finette, Mademoiselle Finette, Josephine!''

Presently he returned, his face distorted, unnerved, dejected. In a toneless voice he said painfully, ''She left without saying a word. I can't believe it!''

Five minutes later, Fandor jumped into a train that took him back to Paris.

23

"State's Evidence"

"**J**uve, I'm stumped." The journalist was resting on the great couch in his friend's study, rue Bonaparte, and summed up the long account of the fruitless inquiry he had made at Dixon's with this assertion:

"I'm at the end of my rope! For two days I haven't stopped a minute. After the night at The Crocodile, which I spent for the most part, as I told you, in search of Loupart, yesterday I spent my day on useless trips. My mind is made up; tonight I shall do no more!"

"A cigarette, Fandor?"

"Thanks."

From the crystal vase where Juve, an inveterate smoker, always kept an ample stock of tobacco, he chose an Egyptian cigarette.

"My dear Juve, it is absolutely necessary to go again to Sèvres and draw a close net around Dixon. He needs watching. Isn't that your opinion?"

"I'm not sure."

Juve thought for a few minutes, then said, "After all, why do you think Dixon should be watched?"

"Why, any number of reasons."

"Such as?"

It was Fandor's turn to be surprised. He had given Juve the account of his visit, expecting that would bring him around to his way of thinking, and now Juve doubted that Dixon could even be a suspect.

"You ask me for particulars. I'm going to reply with generalizations. All in all, what do we know about Dixon? That he was in a certain place and carried Josephine off under our very eyes. Hence he is a friend of Josephine's, which in itself looks suspicious."

"Oh!" protested Juve. "You arrive at your conclusions very quickly, Fandor. Josephine is not an honorable woman. She may know the type of people who haunt night spots, yet who, for all that, need not be murderers."

"Then, Juve, how do you account for the fact that during my visit Dixon kept me from meeting Josephine while pretending to look for her? Isn't that a sign of complicity? Doesn't that show clearly that Josephine, realizing that she is suspect in our eyes, has decided to evade us?"

Juve smiled. "Fandor, you have a prodigious imagination. You impute to Dixon the worst intentions without any proof. He got Josephine away, you say? What makes you think so? If you missed her it must have been due to collusion between them. Why? As far as I can see, Josephine simply picked up an old lover at The Crocodile and went off with him as naturally as possible, preferring not to see the arrest of Loupart or Chaleck. But the next day she simply took French leave of the worthy American, and you may be sure he knew nothing about her going."

Fandor was silent and Juve continued: "That being so, what charges can we bring against Dixon? Merely that he knows Josephine."

"You're right, Juve. Perhaps I went too far with my deductions, but frankly, I don't see what our next step should be. All our trails are crossed. Loupart is in flight, Chaleck has vanished, and as for Josephine, I doubt we'll be seeing her any time soon."

While the journalist was speaking, Juve had remained leaning against the window, watching the passersby.

"Fandor, look at this! By the bus, there. The person who's about to cross."

The journalist burst out, "Well, I'll be damned!"

"You see, Fandor, you must never swear to anything."

"Well, aren't we going to arrest her?"

"Why? Do you think her being in this street is pure co-incidence? Look, she's crossing; she's coming straight here. She's entering the house. In a few minutes Josephine will have climbed my stairs and will be seated cozily in this arm-chair, which I'm getting ready and setting directly in the light."

Fandor couldn't get over his astonishment.

"Did you make an appointment with her?"

"Not at all."

Jean, the detective's servant, came into the room and announced: "There is a lady waiting in the sitting room. She would not give her name."

"Show her in, Jean."

A few moments later Josephine entered.

"Good day, mademoiselle," said Juve pleasantly. "What news have you brought us?"

Loupart's mistress stood in the middle of the room, somewhat taken aback. But Juve put her at ease.

"Sit down, Josephine. You mustn't mind my friend Fandor. He has just been telling me about your friend Dixon."

"You know him, sir?"

"A little," said Fandor. "And you, mademoiselle, have been seeing something of him lately?"

"I happened to meet him at The Crocodile."

"And took a liking to him?"

"We took a liking to each other." She turned to Juve. "I suppose you distrust me for giving you the slip with another man?"

Juve smiled. "You found a good companion and forgot us. There is really nothing to be angry about. Now, won't you tell us what brings you here?"

"Yes, but, Monsieur Juve, you must swear to me that you will never repeat what I am going to tell you."

"It is very serious, then?"

"Monsieur Juve, I'm going to put you in a position to arrest Loupart."

"You are very kind, my dear Josephine, but if the attempt is to succeed no better than the one we made at The Croco-dile—"

"No, no. This time you'll be sure to nab him. Day after tomorrow at two o'clock, Loupart is going with some of his gang to Nogent, 7 rue des Charmilles. He's pulling off a job there."

Juve laughed. "They've been fooling you, Josephine. Isn't that your view, Fandor? Do you think that Loupart would try a heist in broad daylight?"

Eager to persuade him, Josephine gave more details.

"There will be fifteen of them outside a little house whose tenants are away. Some of them will make a crowd to help their mates in case of danger. The Beard is in on it, too."

"And Loupart?"

"Yes, Loupart, I tell you. He'll be wearing a black mask."

"Very well, if we have nothing better to do we'll take a trip to Nogent day after tomorrow, eh, Fandor?"

"As you like, Juve."

"Only remember this, Josephine. If this is another one of your little games, you'll be sorry. There is a way for you to prove that you're acting in good faith. Be at Nogent station at half-past one. If we find Loupart where you say he'll be, we'll arrest him. If we don't find him—"

The detective paused, significantly.

"You'll nab him. Only we can't look as if we met by appointment. No one must suspect that I gave you the tip."

At this point Josephine got up to leave. Her plan had succeeded, and Loupart's business would go ahead safely. She turned at the door and nodded, looking at Fandor.

"Another thing, Loupart doesn't like you. You had better be on your guard."

Juve turned thoughtfully to Fandor. "Strange! Is this woman playing with us or is she in earnest, and did you see how she looked at you when she told us to be on our guard!"

24
A Mysterious Clasp

"**H**ello! Hello!"
                Waking with a start, Juve rushed to the telephone. It was already broad daylight, but the detective had gone to bed very late and had been sleeping deeply.

"Yes, it's me, Juve. The Sûreté? It's you, Monsieur Havard? Yes, I am free. Oh! That's strange. No signs? I understand. Count on me. I'll go there and keep you informed."

Juve dressed in haste, went down to the street, and hailed a taxi.

"To Sèvres, the foot of the hill at Bellevue, and step on it!"

He left the taxi and mounted the slope on foot to Dixon's elegant villa. All was quiet, and if he hadn't had word, the detective would have doubted that he was close to the scene of a crime, or at least an attempted one.

He had hardly entered the grounds when a sergeant came toward him and saluted.

"What's happened?" Juve asked.

"Monsieur Dixon is resting just now, and the doctor has forbidden the least noise."

"Is his condition serious?"

"I think not from what Doctor Plassin says."

"Now, sergeant, tell me everything from the beginning."

The sergeant led Juve to the arbor, where a policeman was seated making out a report. Juve took the paper and read:

We, the undersigned, Dubois, Sergeant in the second squad of foot-police, quartered at Sèvres, together with Constable Verdier, received this morning, June 28th, at 6:35 from M. Olivetti, a businessman, living in Bellevue, the following declaration:

"Having left my home at 6:15 and being on the way to the State Railway to take the 6:42 train, by which I go to work every day, I was passing the slopes of Bellevue, when, being level with Brimborion Park, a little short of the villa number 16, which I hear belongs to M. Dixon, an American boxer, I heard a revolver shot followed by the noise of breaking glass, the pieces falling onto a hard surface, most likely stone.

"Stopping for a moment, I looked to see if anyone was hiding nearby. I saw nothing but heard three more revolver shots in quick succession, seeming to come from Dixon's house. After a few minutes I went near the house and ascertained that the panes of the window on the right side of the front were broken, and that pieces of glass were scattered all over the asphalt terrace in front of the house.

"I decided to ring, but no one opened the door. I then thought that some prowlers had amused themselves by making a ruckus, and I was about to continue to the train when I thought I heard someone moaning inside of the house. Then, fearing there was a mishap or a crime, I ran to the police station and made the above statement in the presence of the sergeant."

Juve turned to the sergeant, who gave further details.

"Constable Verdier and I hurried here immediately. We reached the terrace of the house, but we came to a closed door that we couldn't break down. We shouted loudly and were answered by groans and cries for help coming from the room on the first floor, where the windows had been broken. We then got a ladder and climbed up. I passed my hand inside and worked the latch of the window. We went in and found ourselves in a bedroom in perfect order and in which nothing seemed to have been disturbed."

"And then?" urged Juve.

"I went to the far end of the room and found stretched on the bed a man who seemed to be having violent pains. I later learned that this was Monsieur Dixon, the tenant of the house. He could barely speak or move. His shoulders and arms were out of the sheets, and I could see that there were traces of blood effusion on his shoulders and chest. On a shelf to the right of the bed lay a revolver, the six cartridges of which had recently been fired."

"Ah!" cried Juve. "And then?"

"I thought the first thing to do was to call in a doctor. Monsieur Olivetti consented to go and call Doctor Plassin, who lives nearby. Five minutes later the doctor came, and I took advantage of his presence to send my man to the station."

"Have you been over the house?"

"Not yet, inspector, but there shouldn't be any problems. In turning out the pockets of the victim's clothes we found his keys."

"To bring the doctor into the house, you must have opened the door to him, and therefore had a glimpse of the other rooms in the house—the lobby, the staircase?"

The sergeant shook his head.

"No, inspector. We went up the ladder. I tried to get out of the door of Monsieur Dixon's room but found it was locked. This seemed strange, because the assailant presumably entered by the door."

"By the way, sergeant, are there no servants here? The place seems deserted."

Here Constable Verdier put in a word.

"The American lives here alone except for an old charwoman who comes in before nine. She will probably be here in half an hour as she won't know what's happened."

"Good," said Juve. "Let me know as soon as she comes; wait for her in the garden. As for us," and he turned to the sergeant, "let's go inside."

The two men, armed with Dixon's keys, opened the main entrance to the ground floor. There they found nothing out of the ordinary, but on reaching the first floor, it was clear that someone had been there.

The door of a lumber room stood wide open, and on its floor sheets of paper, letters, and documents lay scattered about. Juve took a candle and, after a brief investigation, exclaimed: "They were after the strongbox."

A large steel safe, built into the wall, had been burst open, and the skillful manner in which it had been done showed clearly the hand of an expert. Juve carefully examined the floor, picked up two or three documents that had evidently been walked on, took some measurements that he jotted down in his notebook, and, without telling the sergeant his conclusions, went downstairs again, paying no attention to Dixon, who was being watched over by Doctor Plassin in the next room.

Verdier, who was guarding the house, came forward and said, "Sir, the doctor says Monsieur Dixon is awake. Would you like to see him?"

Juve at once had the ladder put to the first-story window and went up to the boxer's room. The men's description was correct. No disorder was apparent there. At its far end, on a great brass bed, lay a sturdy individual, his face worn with suffering.

In two words Juve introduced himself to the doctor, then expressed his regrets at Dixon's plight.

"These are only contusions, Monsieur Juve. Serious enough, but nothing more. By the way, Monsieur Dixon owes his life to these exceptional muscles. If it hadn't been for his own strength, his body would now be no more than a shapeless pulp."

Juve pricked up his ears. He had heard stories of bones being snapped and broken under a strain that neither flesh nor muscle could resist. The mysterious death of Lady Beltham immediately came to mind.

"Monsieur Dixon, I'm going to ask you to give me all the details of the tragic night you have been through. You probably dined in Paris last evening?"

"No. I dined at home alone," the sick man said in a fairly firm voice.

"Is that your usual habit?"

"No, but between five and seven I had been training hard

for my match with Joe Sans, which was to have come off tomorrow.''

"Do you think your opponent would have been capable of trying to injure you to keep you out of the ring?"

"No, Joe Sans is a good sportsman. Besides, he lives in Brussels and isn't due in Paris till tomorrow."

"And after dinner, what did you do?"

"I fastened the shutters and doors, came up here, and undressed."

"Are you in the habit of bolting yourself into your room?"

"Yes, I lock my door every evening."

"What time was it when you went to bed?"

"Ten at the latest."

"And then?"

"Then I went to sleep, but in the middle of the night a strange noise woke me up. It sounded like a scratching at my door. I shouted and banged my fist on the wall."

"Why?" asked Juve, surprised.

"I thought the scratching came from rats, so I simply made a noise to frighten them away. Then I fell asleep again."

"And afterward?"

"I woke up again, this time because I heard footsteps on the first-floor landing."

"This time you went to see?"

"I meant to. I was about to get up, and I put out my arm to get my matches and revolver when I suddenly felt a weight on my bed. Then I was tied up and bound like a sausage, my arms pinned to my body! For ten minutes I struggled with all my might against a frightful, mysterious grip that grew tighter."

"A lasso!" suggested Doctor Plassin in a low voice.

"Were you able to determine the nature of the thing that was gripping you?" asked Juve.

"I don't know. I remember feeling a marked sensation of dampness and cold at the touch of the thing."

"A wet lasso, exactly. A rope dipped in water automatically becomes taut," remarked the doctor.

"You had to make a great effort to avoid being crushed or broken?"

"A more than human effort, as the doctor has attested. If

it weren't for my exceptional strength I would have been flattened.''

"Good—good," applauded Juve. "That's exactly it!"

"Really! You think so?" asked the American with a touch of sarcasm.

Juve apologized, smiling. His enthusiasm meant no more than that the statements of the victim coincided with the theories he had formed. And, indeed, he saw clearly in the unsuccessful attempt on the American and the murder of Lady Beltham a common technique, the same process. Due to his robust physique, the American was only slightly hurt, but the hapless woman had been totally crushed.

The similarity of the two crimes allowed Juve to make further inductions. He concluded that it was no coincidence that Dixon had met Josephine at The Crocodile two nights before, and the presence of both Chaleck and Loupart in that establishment was still less accidental. He felt pleased at the thought that he was almost certain who the villains must be. They wanted to get rid of Dixon, that was obvious, and by a process still unknown to Juve, but one that he would soon discover. They had rendered the boxer helpless while they robbed him.

"Did you have a large amount of money in your safe?" he asked.

The American gave a violent start.

"They've robbed me! Tell me, tell me quickly!"

Juve nodded in the affirmative. Dixon stammered feebly, "Four thousand pounds! They've taken four thousand pounds from me! I got the money a few days ago!"

"Gently, gently!" observed the doctor. "You'll make yourself feverish and I'll have to stop the interview."

"I only want a few moments more, Doctor," said Juve. "It's important." Then, turning to Dixon, he continued: "How did your struggle with the mysterious pressure end?"

"After about ten minutes I felt its grip relaxing. In a short while I was free. I heard nothing more, but I felt such a sharp pain that I fell back in bed and either fell asleep or fainted."

"Then you did not get up at all?"

"No."

"And the door from your room to the landing remained locked all night?"

"Yes, all night."

"How about this broken glass in your window? Those revolver shots at six in the morning?"

"I fired from my bed to attract someone's attention."

"I thought as much," said Juve as he went down on all fours and proceeded to examine the carpeting between the bed and the door, a distance of some seven feet. The carpet showed no trace of anything unusual, but on a white bearskin rug the detective noted tufts of fur glued together in places, as if something moist and sticky had passed over it. He cut off one of these tufts and put it carefully between the pages of his notebook. He then went to the door, which was hidden by a velvet curtain. He could not suppress a cry of amazement. In the lower panel of the door a round hole of about six or eight inches in diameter had been drilled. It was four inches above the floor and might have been made for a cat.

"Did you have that hole made in the door?" asked Juve.

"No. I don't know what it is," replied the American.

"Neither do I," rejoined Juve, "but I have an idea."

Doctor Plassin was jubilant.

"There you are!" he cried. "A lasso! And it was thrust in through that hole."

Through the window Verdier called, "Monsieur, the charwoman is coming."

Juve looked at his watch.

"Half-past nine. I'll see her in a minute."

25
The Trap

"Twelve o'clock! Damn it! I have just enough time to keep my appointment with Josephine."

Using a short cut, Juve was going down Belleville hill as fast as he could, past the Sèvres school. He cast a mocking glance toward the little police station which stood on one side of the street.

"Pity," he murmured, "that I can't escort my friends to that delightful country house."

Then he increased his pace. He was getting angry.

"I told Fandor to be at Nogent station, exactly at one-thirty. It's now five past twelve and I'm still at Sèvres. Things are getting complicated. I'll take the tram to Versailles's gate. From there I'll drive to Nogent station in a taxi."

He put this plan into execution and was lucky enough to find a place in the Louvre-Versailles tram.

"All things considered, I haven't wasted my morning," he said to himself. "Poor Dixon! He was lucky to get off so easily. It seems Josephine told the truth when she said he wasn't one of the gang."

Juve reflected a while, then added: "Only it looks as if that damned Josephine put her friends up to the job."

At the St. Cloud gate the tram came to a stop and Juve got down, hailed a taxi, and told the driver: "Nogent station, and hurry."

The driver nodded assent, Juve got in, and the vehicle started. The taxi had hardly been going five minutes when Juve became impatient.

"Quicker! Is this the best you can do?"

Nettled, the man replied, "I don't want to get a ticket."

Juve laughed.

"Never mind, I'm from police headquarters."

The magical word took effect. From that moment, despite the frantic signals of policemen, the driver tore along at full speed and soon reached the square in front of Nogent station.

"It's only one forty-five—Fandor should just be getting here."

Juve, indeed, had only just settled with his driver when Fandor popped up from the waiting room.

"Well, Juve! Anything new?"

The detective smiled.

"Any number of things. But I'll tell you later. Where's Josephine?"

"Not here yet."

"Damn!"

"That confirms my suspicions, eh, Juve?"

"Somewhat. I'll be surprised if we do see her."

The detective led the journalist away, and the two went for a walk on a deserted boulevard beside the railroad.

"Fandor, this is the time to draw up a plan of action. Do you remember the directions Josephine gave us?"

"Vaguely."

"Well, we're now going to the neighborhood of the rue des Charmilles. It is number seven that Loupart and his gang are to loot, according to Josephine. Yesterday afternoon I sent my men to look at the street; this is how they described it to me. It's a kind of cul-de-sac; the house we're concerned with is the last one on the right. It's very humble, and the tenants are away. Charmilles Lane is very quiet, so the place is well suited for the job, at least that's Michel's opinion.

"Oh, I forgot one thing; around the house there's a fairly large garden with high walls. So even if the burglars discover us they probably couldn't get out the back way."

"And what's your plan, Juve?"

"It's very simple. We're going to the entrance of the rue

des Charmilles and wait there. When our men get here I'll try to stop Loupart. No doubt there'll be a struggle, but in the meantime you must bellow with all your might: 'Murder,' 'Help.' I trust that help will reach us.''

"Then you haven't any plainclothesmen here?"

"No. I don't want my superiors to know about this."

The two men walked in silence along an empty side street, where Juve stopped in a shady corner and drew out his Browning.

"Do as I do, Fandor," he said, getting ready. "I smell powder in the air."

Juve was about to move on when a tremendous uproar broke out: "Help! Help!"

Juve seized Fandor by the arm.

"Take the left side!"

They had just reached the corner of the street where the house was when a crowd of people came in sight, rushing toward them, yelling and shouting. Juve and Fandor saw a man fleeing at full speed in front of them, his face hidden by a black mask! Behind him two other men were running, also masked, but with gray velvet. In the crowd following were grocers' assistants, workmen of all kinds—even a Nogent policeman.

"Help! Murder! Arrest him!"

The fleeing man was threatening the crowd with an enormous revolver.

"Look out!" shouted Juve. "Loupart is mine! You tackle the others!"

Suddenly catching sight of the detective, the leader slowed down.

"Get out of the way!" he cried, brandishing his revolver.

"Stop, or I fire!" said Juve.

"Fire, then," he rejoined, leaping toward the detective. The thief aimed his revolver and fired twice.

With a quick movement Juve leaped aside. The bullets must have brushed him, but luckily he wasn't wounded. He threw himself on Loupart, seized him by the collar, and tried to pin him down.

"Let me go! I'll get you—"

For a moment Juve felt the cold muzzle of the weapon on

his neck. Then, with a supreme effort, he forced the outlaw's hands down and, aiming his revolver, fired.

"Help! I—I—"

A gush of blood welled up from the ruffian's collar. He turned twice, then fell heavily to the ground.

In the meantime Fandor was struggling with the two men in the gray masks. Juve was about to go to his assistance when the crowd now made a rush and the detective became the central point of a furious encounter: blows and kicks rained on him. He succumbed to the force of numbers.

It was now Fandor's turn to help his friend, and he was about to join the fray when he stood rooted to the spot in utter amazement. A little beyond the groups of struggling men he caught sight of someone standing beside a tripod on which was placed a contrivance he did not at once identify. The man seemed greatly amused. He was watching the scene laughing and showed no desire to intervene.

"Great! Great! This'll make a tremendous film!"

Fandor understood.

His head bandaged and his arm in a sling, Juve answered the superintendent of police in a shaky voice.

"No, superintendent, I realized nothing. It is monstrous! I asked in the most perfect good faith. I did not fire till I had been fired at three times."

"You didn't notice the strange getup of the burglars? And of the policemen? Of that poor actor, Bonardin, whom you half killed?"

Juve shook his head.

"I didn't have time to notice details. I want you to understand, superintendent, how things came about, to realize how the trap was laid for me. . . . I came to Nogent, sure that I was about to face dangerous criminals. I was to encounter them at such an hour, in such a street. I was given their description: They would have their faces masked and come out of a certain house. And it all happened as described. I hadn't gone ten paces in the street when, sure enough, I saw people rushing toward me yelling 'Help!' I saw men in masks; do you think I had time to check the details of their costumes? Certainly not! So I spring at the throat of the fugitive. He has a revolver and fires. How could I know the gun was only loaded with blanks? He, a film actor in a scene, takes me for another, acting the part of a policeman. He fires at me, and I retaliate.''

"And you half kill him.''

"For which I am exceedingly sorry. But nothing led me to suspect a trap.''

"You're lucky you didn't hurt anyone else. How did it all end?''

"The actors, naturally enough, were furious with me, and they were letting me know it when the real policemen arrived and rescued me. Everything was cleared up when I identified myself. While they were taking me to the station, the actor Bonardin was being carried to the nearest house, a convent, I believe.''

"Yes, the Convent of the Ladies of St. Clotilde.''

The trap had been well devised, and Juve was not wrong in saying that anyone in his place would have been taken in by it. And so while the detective was detained at the station, Fandor, after a long and careful interrogation, returned to Paris in a state of deep dejection.

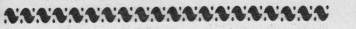

26
With Bonardin, the Actor

Fandor was passing Rokin College in the place d'Anvers when he heard someone calling him.

"Monsieur Fandor! Monsieur Fandor!"

It was Josephine, breathless and panting, her bright eyes glowing.

Fandor turned, astonished.

"What's up?"

Josephine paused a second, then, taking Fandor's hand familiarly, drew him into the square, which at this time of day was almost deserted.

"Oh, it's something out of the ordinary, I can assure you. I'm going to astonish you!"

"You've done that already. The mere sight of you—"

"You thought I'd been arrested, didn't you?"

Fandor nodded.

"Well, it's your Juve who's behind bars!"

Contrary to Josephine's expectation, Fandor did not seem surprised.

"Come now, Josephine, that's a likely story! Juve arrested? On what grounds?"

Josephine began an incoherent story.

"I tell you they squabbled like rag-pickers! 'You make justice ridiculous,' shouted Fuselier. 'No one has the right to commit such blunders!' Well, they went on like that for a quarter of an hour. And then Fuselier rang and two police officers came and he said: 'Arrest that man there!' pointing to Juve. And your friend the detective was obliged to go with them. Only as he left the room he gave Fuselier such a look! Believe me, between those two it is war to the death from now on.''

When she had finished Fandor asked in a calm voice, "And how did you get away, Josephine?''

"Oh, Monsieur Fuselier was very nice. 'It's you again?' he said when he saw me. 'To be sure it is,' I answered, 'and I'm glad to meet you again, Monsieur.' Then he began talking about the cinema business. I told him what I knew about it, what I told you. Loupart stuffed me up with his tale of a trap. As sure as my name's Josephine, I believed what he told me.''

Fandor gave her a penetrating look.

"And how about the Dixon business?''

Josephine blushed and said in a low voice, "Oh, the Dixon business. As to that—we are very good pals, Dixon and I. I went to see him yesterday afternoon. He's taken a fancy to me. He promised to keep me in luxury. Ah, if I dared,'' sighed the girl.

"You would do well to leave Loupart.''

"Leave Loupart? Especially now that Juve is out of the picture, Loupart will be the king of Paris!''

"Do you think your lover will attach much weight to Juve's arrest? Won't he suspect it's a put-up job?''

"A put-up job! How could it be? Why, I saw Juve being led away with my own two eyes.''

The growing hubbub of the boys hawking the evening news drew near the place d'Anvers. Instinctively Fandor, followed by Josephine, went toward them. On the boulevard he bought a paper.

"There, you see!'' cried Josephine triumphantly. "Here it is in print, so it is true!''

This notice appeared in bold headlines: "AMAZING DEVELOPMENT IN THE AFFAIR OF THE OUTLAWS OF LA CHAPELLE. DETECTIVE JUVE UNDER LOCK AND KEY.''

When he met Josephine in the place d'Anvers, Fandor was on the way to the rue des Abesses, where Bonardin occupied a nice little suite of three rooms, tastefully decorated and comfortably furnished.

The actor's shoulder was in a cast. Juve's bullet had broken his collarbone, but the doctor said that with a few days' rest he would be fine.

"Monsieur Fandor, I am very sorry about Monsieur Juve. Do you think if I were to declare my intention not to press charges—"

Fandor cut the man short.

"Let justice take its course, Monsieur Bonardin. There will be time later on."

Although M. Bonardin was only twenty-five, he already had an outstanding reputation. By hard work he had come rapidly to the forefront and was fast becoming one of the best interpreters of modern comedy.

"My dream," he exclaimed to Fandor, "is one day to attain the fame of my masters—men like Tazzide, Gémier, Valgrand, and Du-mény."

"You knew Valgrand?" asked Fandor.

Bonardin smiled.

"Yes, we were great friends. When I made my first appearance at the theater, after the Conservatoire, Valgrand was my model, my master. You wouldn't remember, Monsieur Fandor, but I played the lover in the famous play *La Toche Sanglante*, for which Valgrand had made himself up exactly like Gurn, the murderer of Lord Beltham. You must have heard of the case?"

Fandor pretended to tax his memory.

"Yes, of course. I do recall certain incidents, but won't you refresh my memory?"

Bonardin needed no further encouragement.

"Valgrand, on the first night of his presentation of Gurn, was quite worn out and left the theater very late. He did not come back! For the second performance his understudy took his part. The following day they sent to his rooms; he had not been there for two days. Three days after opening night Valgrand reappeared."

"Please go on. This is very interesting!"

"Valgrand came back, but he had gone mad. He managed to get to his dressing room after taking the wrong door 'I don't know a single word of my part,' he confessed to me. I comforted him as best I could, but he flung himself down on the couch and shook his head helplessly. 'I have been very ill, Bonardin.' Suddenly he demanded, 'Where is Charlot?'

"Charlot was his dresser. I remembered that Charlot had not returned to the theater since his master's disappearance. I did not want to mention this to him for fear it might upset him still more, so I advised my old friend to wait for me till the end of the play and let me keep him company. I intended to take him home and call a doctor. Valgrand agreed. I had to leave him soon afterward. They were calling me—it was my cue. When I returned Valgrand had vanished: He had left the theater. We were not to see him again!''

"A sad affair," commented Fandor.

Bonardin continued his narrative: "Shortly afterward in a deserted house in the rue Messier, near boulevard Arago, the police found the body of a murdered man. The corpse was easily identified; it was Charlot, Valgrand's dresser.

"How had he come to be there? The house had no concierge. The owner, an old peasant, knew nothing."

"Well, what did you make of it?" asked Fandor.

"My theory is that Valgrand murdered his dresser, for some reason unknown to us. Then, overcome by his crime, he went mad and committed suicide. Of that there is no doubt."

"Oh!" muttered Fandor, a little taken aback by this unexpected assertion.

The journalist, though he had closely followed the actor's account, was far from drawing the same conclusions. In fact, Gurn, Lord Beltham's murderer, whom Fandor believed to be Fantômas, had managed to get Valgrand executed in his place. The Valgrand who came back to the theater three days after the execution was not the real one, but the man who had taken his place—Gurn, the criminal, Gurn/Fantômas. Ah! that was a stroke of Fantômas genius! If Valgrand's disappearance had coincided with Gurn's execution, suspicions might have been raised. Gurn/Fantômas then found it necessary to show Valgrand living to witnesses, so that they could swear that the real Valgrand had not died instead of Gurn.

But Valgrand was an actor. Gurn/Fantômas was not! Not enough of one, at least, to attempt to take the place on the boards of such a consummate player, such a famous tragedian.

"And that was the end?" asked Fandor.

"The end, no!" declared the actor. "Valgrand was married and had a son. As is often the case with artists, the Valgrand marriage was not a success, and Madame, a talented singer, separated from her husband and went abroad.

"About a year after these sad occurrences I had a visit from her. On her way through Paris she had come to draw the allowance made her by her husband, to supply not only her own wants, but those of their son, of whom she had custody. Madame Valgrand chatted with me for hours. I told her everything I've just told you, and it seemed to me that she attached little importance to what I said.

"Not that she threw doubts on my statements, but she kept saying, 'That is not like him; I know Valgrand would never have behaved in such a way!'

"But I never could get her to say exactly what she thought. Some weeks after this first visit I saw her again. Matters were getting complicated. There was no certificate of her husband's death. The accountants made his absence a pretext. She could no longer draw a cent of her allowance, and yet people knew that Valgrand had left a pretty large amount. It was in the bank or with a lawyer, I forget which. You are aware, Monsieur Fandor, that when there are problems with the settling of accounts, or questions of inheritance or wills, there is no end to them."

"That's a fact," replied Fandor.

"We must believe," went on Bonardin, "that the matter was important to Madame Valgrand because she refused fine offers from abroad and settled in Paris, living on her savings. She evidently had a double object: to recover the inheritance for her son little René and also to get at the truth about her husband's fate.

"She evidently cherished the hope that her husband was not guilty of the dresser's murder, that perhaps he wasn't even dead, that he would get over his madness if they ever managed to find him. In short, Monsieur Fandor, some six or seven months ago, when I had stopped thinking of these events, I found myself face to face with Madame Valgrand. I had some difficulty recognizing her because she was no longer dressed like the smart Parisian woman. Her hair was plastered down and drawn back tightly; her clothes were plain and humble; her dress almost neglected. No doubt the poor woman had experienced cruel disappointments.

" 'Good day, Madame Valgrand,' I cried, moving toward her with outstretched hands. She stopped me with a gesture.

" 'Hush,' she breathed, 'there is no Madame Valgrand now. I am a companion.' And the unhappy woman explained that in order to earn her living she had been forced to accept an inferior position as reader and housekeeper to a rich lady."

"And to whom did Madame Valgrand go as companion?"

"To an Englishwoman, I believe. But the name escapes me."

"Madame Valgrand wished, you say, her identity remain unknown? Do you know what name she assumed?"

"Yes—Madame Raymond."

After a few minutes Fandor left the actor and could be seen hurrying down the rue Lepic.

27
The Mother Superior

"**T**he mother superior, please?"

The door shut automatically, and Fandor found himself in the inner court of the small convent facing a nun who gazed in alarm at the unexpected guest.

"Can I see the mother superior?" the journalist persisted.

"Well, sir, yes—but no, I think not."

The nun evidently did not know what to say. Finally making up her mind she pointed to a passage, and, drawing aside to let the journalist pass, said: "Be good enough to go in there and wait a few moments."

Fandor was ushered into a large, plain, austere room. Long, white curtains hung at the windows, and in front of the half-dozen armchairs lay tiny rugs made of matting; the floor, highly waxed, was extremely slippery. The journalist looked curiously at the walls, which were decorated with religious figures and prints. Above the chimney hung a great ebony crucifix. Except for the noise outside—the sound of trains and automobiles—and the aroma of food being cooked, he might have been hundreds of miles away from the rest of the world.

Bonardin, taken in at the time of his accident by the sisters of the rue Charmille, had received from them the first aid his condition required. As he had left them without a word of thanks, he had begged Fandor to return and give them, on his behalf, a fifty-franc bill for the poor.

After a few minutes the door opened and a nun appeared. She greeted Fandor with a slight movement of the head; the journalist bowed deferentially.

"Have I the honor of speaking to the mother superior?" he asked.

"Our Mother sends her blessings," murmured the nun, "but she is unable to receive you at this moment. May I help you?"

"I bring the news of Bonardin, sister."

The nun clasped her hands.

"Good news, I hope! How is the poor young man doing?"

"As well as can be expected. The bullet was extracted without trouble by the doctors."

"I shall thank St. Comus, the patron saint of surgeons. And his assailant? Surely he will be justly punished?"

Fandor smiled.

"His assailant was the victim of a terrible misconception. He is a most upright man."

"Then I will pray to St. Yves, the patron saint of advocates, to get him out of his difficulty."

"Well," cried Fandor, "since you have so many saints at your command, sister, perhaps you could point out to me one who might favor the efforts of the police in their struggle against crime."

The nun smiled and rejoined: "You might try St. George, the patron saint of warriors." Then becoming serious again, the sister ended the interview. "Our mother superior will be touched when I tell her how kind you have been in coming here to us."

"Allow me, sister," interrupted Fandor. "My mission is not over yet."

Here the journalist discreetly proffered the note.

"This is from Monsieur Bonardin, for the poor."

The nun was profuse in her thanks and, looking at Fandor with a touch of mischief, said: "You may smile, sir, if I say I shall thank St. Martin, the patron saint of the charitable. In any case, I shall do it with my whole heart."

The soft sound of a bell came from the distance. The sister

instinctively turned her head and looked through the windows
at the inner cloister of the convent.

"The bell calls you, no doubt, sister?" Fandor inquired.

"Yes. It is time for Vespers."

Fandor, followed by the sister, left the parlor and reached
the outer gate. The caretaker was about to open it for him
when he stopped suddenly. Moving at a measured pace, one
behind the other, the ladies of the community crossed the
courtyard, going toward the chapel at the far end of the garden.

"Sister," Fandor asked anxiously, "who is that nun walking at the head?"

"That is our holy mother superior."

Fandor was lucky enough to find a taxi as he left the little
convent; he was immersed in such deep reflection that when
the taxi let him off he was surprised to find himself in the
rue Bonaparte. He had intended to call on Bonardin and expected to be in Montmarte.

"Where did I tell you to go?" he asked the driver. The
man looked at his fare in amazement.

"To the address you gave me, I suppose."

Fandor did not reply, but paid his fare.

"Heaven must have inspired me," he thought. "To be sure
I wanted to let Bonardin know I had done what he asked, but
it turns out I should have gone after what I discovered at the
convent."

The journalist remained motionless on the pavement without seeming to feel the jostling of the passersby. He stood
there with his eyes fixed on the ground, his mind lost in a
dream. He had unconsciously gone back several years, to his
mysterious childhood, stormy and restless. He went over
again in thought the affair that had once more brought him
so intimately into Juve's life: the abominable crime in the
Cité Frochot, in which Chaleck and Loupart were involved,
and behind them Fantômas—the crime of which the victim—
as Juve had clearly established—was none other than Lady—

He quickly entered the house and rushed up the stairs, but
stopped on the landing.

"What have I come here for?" he thought. "If I am to
believe the papers, Juve is under lock and key. It must be

instinct that guides me. I feel that I am going to see Juve. Besides, I must."

He did not ring. He enjoyed the privilege of a key which allowed him to enter Juve's place at will. He entered and went straight to the study. It was empty. He then cried out: "Juve! Many things have happened since I had the pleasure of seeing you! Be good enough to let me into your office. I have two words to say to you."

But Fandor's words resounded in the silence of the apartment. After this summons he went into the office and ensconced himself in an armchair. Clearly Fandor was sure his friend had heard him. And he was not wrong! Seconds later, lifting a curtain that concealed a secret entrance to the study, Juve appeared.

"You sounded as if you knew I was here!"

The two men looked at each other and burst into peals of laughter.

"So you understood it was all a sham intended to make our opponents believe that for a time I was powerless to hurt them. What do you think of my notion?"

"First rate," replied Fandor. "The more so that the fair Josephine 'saw with her own eyes' some officers taking you off to prison."

"Everybody believes it, don't they?"

"Everybody."

"Look here. Just now you spoke as though you knew I was here?"

Fandor smiled.

"The odor of hot smoke is easily distinguished from the dankness of cold tobacco."

Juve approved.

"Well done, Fandor. Here, for your pains, roll a cigarette and let's talk. Have you anything new to tell me?"

"Yes—and a lot, too!"

Fandor related the talk he had had with Bonardin about Valgrand, the actor, and the information about Mme. Valgrand, alias Mme. Raymond.

"This is one more riddle to solve," Juve said. "I still adhere to the theory that Josephine, some months ago, was brought into the household of Lady Beltham, whose body I discovered at Cité Frochot and later identified.''

Fandor sprang up, placing both of his hands on Juve's shoulders.

"Lady Beltham is not dead, she's alive!" he exclaimed. "As surely as my name is Fandor, the mother superior of the convent at Nogent is Lady Beltham."

28
An Old Paralytic

At the far end of the rue de Rome Fandor stopped. "After all," he thought, "maybe I'm heading straight for a trap. Who sent me the letter? Who is this Monsieur Mahon? I've never heard of him. Why this mysterious phrase: 'Come, if you take any interest in the affairs of Lady B— and F—.' Oh, if only I could consult Juve!"

But for the past two weeks, since the affair of Nogent and the almost incredible discovery he had made that Lady Beltham was still alive, Fandor had not seen Juve. He had been to the Sûreté a number of times, but Juve had once more vanished.

Fandor stopped before a private house on the boulevard Pereire North. He went in through the outer hall and reached the porter's lodge.

"Madame, do you have you a tenant here named Mahon?" The concierge came forward.

"Monsieur Mahon? Yes, of course—fifth floor on the right."

"Thank you. I would like to ask you a few questions about him. I have come to negotiate an insurance policy for him, and I would like to know about the value of the furniture in his rooms. What sort of man is this Monsieur Mahon? About how old is he?"

Fandor had, by pure professional instinct, found the best

device in the world. There is not a concierge who has not enlightened an insurance agent.

"Why, Monsieur Mahon has lived here less than a month. He can hardly be very well off because when he moved in I didn't see any fine furniture go up. For that matter, I believe he is an old cavalry officer, and nobody makes a fortune in the army nowadays."

"That's true enough," agreed Fandor.

"Anyway, he is a very charming man, an ideal lodger. To begin with, he is infirm, almost paralyzed in both legs. I don't believe he ever goes out. And he never has any visitors except for two young fellows who are serving in the army."

"Are they with him now?"

"No, sir. They never come till three or four in the afternoon."

Fandor slipped a coin into the woman's hand and went upstairs. He rang at the door and was surprised to hear a strange, soft, rolling sound.

"Oh, I know," he thought; "the poor man must move about his rooms in a rubber-tired wheelchair."

He wasn't mistaken. The door had barely opened when he caught sight of a distinguished old man seated in a wheelchair. The invalid greeted the journalist pleasantly.

"Monsieur Fandor?"

"The same, sir."

M. Mahon pushed his chair forward and motioned to his visitor to come in.

Fandor entered a room in which the curtains were drawn and the place was flooded with electric lights, even though it was the middle of the afternoon. Was it a trap? The journalist instinctively hesitated in the doorway. But behind him a cordial voice called:

"Come in, you idiot!"

The door clicked behind him and the invalid, getting out of his chair, burst into a fit of laughter.

"Juve! Juve!"

"In the flesh!"

"What farce are you playing here? Why this lit-up room?"

"All for very good reasons. If you will be kind enough to take a seat, I'll explain everything."

Staring at Juve, Fandor fell into a chair.

"When you came back two weeks ago and told me that unlikely yarn about Lady Beltham being alive, I decided to try new methods. First of all, I became a cavalry officer. Then I got this wheelchair and moved into this apartment."

As Juve paused, Fandor, more and more amazed, questioned, "But your reason for all this!"

"Just wait! The day after the Dixon business I put three of my best men on the track of the American. I had a notion he would want to see Josephine again, and I was not mistaken. She came back to justify herself in his eyes. The story ended as might have been foreseen. Michel, who brought me the news, said that Josephine had agreed to become Dixon's mistress."

"You don't say!"

"Oh, that didn't surprise me. Michel made arrangements to learn all the details. Josephine is to live at thirty-three C in boulevard Pereire South. That is, to the right of the railway line, fourth floor. Here we are at twenty-four B boulevard Pereire North—to the left of the railway, fifth floor, and just opposite."

"And what does old Monsieur Mahon do, Juve?"

Juve smiled.

"You'll soon see," he said.

He settled himself in the wheelchair again, drew a heavy rug over his knees, and once more became the old invalid.

"My dear friend, will you open the door for me?"

Fandor laughingly complied, and Juve wheeled himself into another room.

"You see, I have plenty of air here thanks to this balcony. Would you be good enough to pass me that telescope?"

Juve pointed it toward the far end of boulevard Pereire, in the direction of Poste Maillot.

"Mademoiselle Josephine has lately had a craze for keeping her nails polished."

"But you're not looking toward the house opposite; you're looking in another direction!"

Juve laid his telescope on his knees and laughed.

"I expected you to make that remark. See, the glass at the end is only for show; inside there's a whole system of prisms.

With this perspective you see not in front of you but on one side. In other words, when I point it at the far end of the boulevard, what I'm really looking at is the house opposite."

Fandor was about to congratulate his friend on this new specimen of his ingenuity, but Juve didn't give him time. He startled the journalist by suddenly asking him: "Tell me, do you love the army?"

"Why?"

"Because I think those two soldiers you see over there are coming."

"To see you," added Fandor.

"How do you know?"

"From your concierge."

"You pumped her?"

"I did. I got her to talk a bit about that excellent Monsieur Mahon."

Juve laughed. "Confound you!" he said.

With a quick movement Fandor at the detective's request, drew back the wheelchair and closed the window.

"You understand," explained Juve, "there is nothing wrong with my neighbors knowing that two soldiers come to visit me. But I don't want a third party to hear what they say to me." There was a ring at the apartment door. "Open it, Fandor. I don't leave my cripple's chair for them; people can see through the curtains."

Shown in by Fandor, the soldiers shook hands with Juve and took seats opposite him.

"Do you recognize Michel and Léon?"

"Oh, perfectly!" cried Fandor. "But why this disguise?"

"Because no one pays any attention to uniforms. There are soldiers everywhere, and also it's not easy to recognize a civilian suddenly appearing in uniform. What's new, Michel?"

"Something pretty serious, sir. According to your instructions we've been shadowing the mother superior of the Nogent convent."

"Well, what have you discovered?"

"Every Tuesday evening she leaves Nogent and goes to Paris."

"Where?"

"To one of the branches of her religious order in the boulevard Jourdan."

"Number one hundred eighty?"

Michel was dumbfounded.

"Yes, sir. You knew?"

"No," said Juve coldly. "What does she do at this branch?"

"There are four or five old nuns there. The mother superior spends Tuesday night there and on Wednesday goes back to Nogent at about one in the afternoon."

"And you know no more than that?"

"No, sir. Should we go on with the shadowing?"

"No, it's not worthwhile. Return to the prefecture and report to Monsieur Havard."

When the two men had left, Fandor turned to Juve. "What do you make of it?" he asked.

Juve shrugged his shoulders.

"Michel is an idiot. That house has two exits: one to the boulevard, the other to a vacant lot that leads to the fortifications. The mother superior, or Lady Beltham, goes there to change her dress and then hurries to some prearranged meeting elsewhere. The house at Neuilly will need watching."

29
Through the Window

"**W**hat a splendid fellow! He can always be counted on. A friendship like his is rare, indeed."

Fandor had just left Juve, and the detective couldn't help being moved as he thought of the journalist's devotion. He was still in his wheelchair. Turning skillfully, he went back to the balcony and to his observation post.

Evening was coming on. After a fine day the sky had become leaden and overcast: a storm was threatening. Juve swore.

"I won't see much this evening. This confounded Josephine is so sentimental that she loves dreaming in the twilight at her window without turning on the lights. Damn her!"

Juve had armed himself with his telescope. He apparently leveled it at Porte Maillot, and in that way he could see something of Josephine's movements.

"Flowers on the chimney and on the piano! Expecting her lover probably!"

Suddenly he started up in his chair.

"Ah! someone has rung her bell. She's going toward the door."

A minute passed. In the front rooms Juve could no longer see anyone. Josephine must be receiving a visitor. A few minutes went by. There was a heavy downpour, and Juve was forced to leave the balcony. When he resumed his watch he could not suppress an exclamation of surprise.

"Ah, if he would only turn! This damned rain prevents me from seeing clearly. The brute! Why won't he turn! There, he's put his bag on a chair. His initials must be on it, but I can't read them. Yet the height of the man . . . his gestures . . . It's he, sure enough, it's Chaleck!"

Juve suddenly abandoned his lookout, wheeled his chair to the back room of the suite, and grabbed the telephone.

"Hello! Give me the prefecture. It's Juve speaking. Send detectives Léon and Michel to number thirty-three C boulevard Pereire South at once. They are to wait at the door of the house and arrest, as they come out, the two people I marked as numbers fourteen and fifteen. Tell them to hurry.

"Chaleck won't leave right away if he's come to see Josephine; no doubt he has important things to say. Léon and Michel will arrive in time to nab him first and Josephine after. And tomorrow, when I have them handcuffed before me, I'll be damned if I don't manage to get the truth out of them."

Juve went back to his lookout.

"Oh, they seem very lively, both of them; the talk must be serious. Josephine doesn't look pleased. She seems to disagree with what Chaleck is saying. One would think he was giving her orders. No! she's down on her knees. A declaration of love! After Loupart and Dixon, it's that infernal doctor's turn!"

Juve watched the young woman and the mysterious and elusive Chaleck for a little longer.

"Ah! that's what I was afraid of! Chaleck is leaving and Léon and Michel haven't come yet!"

Juve hesitated. Should he go down, rush to the boulevard, and try to collar the man? That wasn't possible. Juve lived on the fifth floor, so he had one more story than Chaleck to get down. Then there was the railroad tracks between the two houses. Chaleck would have plenty of time to disappear.

"But luckily he's left his bag," Juve reassured himself, "and if I am not mistaken, that's his cane on the chair. Therefore he expects to come back."

Powerless to act, Juve watched as Chaleck left. He soon

appeared at the door of Josephine's house and went out. Juve
followed him with his eyes, extremely peeved. Would he ever
again find such a good opportunity of laying hands on the
criminal?

Chaleck vanished around the corner, and Juve again took
to watching Josephine. The young woman did not appear to
be upset by her recent visitor. She sat, her elbows on the
table, listlessly turning the pages of a book.

"He's obviously coming back," thought Juve, "or he
wouldn't have left his things there. I'll have him in a few
days at the latest."

Juve was about to leave his post when he saw Josephine
raise her head as if she was listening to some indefinable,
mysterious noise.

"What's going on?" Juve asked himself. "She can't be
watching for Chaleck's return already."

Then he started.

"Oh! oh!"

He had just seen Josephine spring toward the window at a
single bound. The young woman gazed steadily in front of
her, her arms outstretched. She seemed in a state of abject
terror. There was no mistaking her motions. She was panic-
stricken, panting, trembling in all her limbs. Juve, who could
see every movement of the hapless woman, felt a cold sweat
break out on his forehead.

"What's the matter with her? There's nobody in the room,
I see nothing! What could be frightening her to that extent?
Oh, my God!"

Forgetting all precautions, all the theatrics he had prepared
so carefully for the neighbors' benefit, he sprang to his feet,
abandoning his wheelchair. His hands clenched on the rail of
the balcony while, spellbound by the sight before his eyes,
he leaned over the rail as if in a frantic desire to fling himself
to the young woman's rescue. Josephine had now climbed
out onto the windowsill and was standing on the ledge, holding the rail of the balcony with one hand, her body flung
backward as if mad with terror.

"What's happening?"

Josephine, with a desperate cry, had let go of the rail and
flung herself into space. Juve saw the young woman's body

spin in the air and heard the dull thud it made as it hit the ground.

"This is monstrous!"

Beside himself, Juve tore down the stairs, past the concierge, who seemed on the verge of fainting when she saw the supposed paralytic darting down the stairs. He went around boulevard Pereire, ran along the railway line, and, panting, got to the side of the unfortunate Josephine. When Juve got there a ring of people had already formed around her. The detective pushed some of them aside roughly, knelt down beside the woman's body, and put his ear to her chest.

"Dead? No!"

A faint groan came from her lips. Juve realized that, miraculously, in the course of her fall Josephine had struck the outer branches of one of the trees that fringed the boulevard. This had broken the shock, but both of her legs were broken and one of her arms hung lifeless.

"Quick!" commanded Juve. "A cab; she has to get to the hospital."

As soon as Josephine had been taken care of, Juve, remembering why he was here, asked himself: "What could have happened? What was it she was trying so desperately to escape? I saw the whole room, and there was no one with her. Is is possible she was hallucinating?"

30
Uncle and Nephew

"So, Uncle, you have decided to live at Neuilly?"

"Oh, it's quite settled. Your aunt finds the place charming, and besides, it would be so pleasant to have a garden. Also, the land in this neighborhood is certain to become more valuable. Purchasing a house here would be a good speculation!"

The stout man beamed as he uttered the word "speculation." The mere sight of him suggested the small tradesman grown rich by dint of long and arduous years of toil, retired from business and prone to imagine he is a man of genius.

Compared with him, the young man he called nephew, slim, elaborately elegant, his little mustache carefully curled, gave the impression of someone who had just come out of a tailor's shop and wanted to be taken for a man of the world. Evidently the nephew courted the uncle and flattered him.

"You are right, land speculations are very sure and quite profitable. So you wrote to the caretaker of the house to let you see it?"

"I did, and he answered, 'Come today or tomorrow. I shall be at your disposal.' That's why I sent you word to come and go with me. Since you are the sole heir to my fortune—"

"Oh, Uncle, you may be sure—"

The Madeleine tram, where the two men were talking

aloud, paying little attention to the amused other passengers, pulled up in the place de l'Eglise at Neuilly.

"Let's get off. The boulevard Inkermann begins here."

Panting and gasping like a man whose weight has made all physical exercise a burden, the uncle lowered himself off the tram. The young man sprang to his side. After five minutes' walk the two men were in front of Lady Beltham's house, the identical house Juve and Fandor had previously visited.

"You see, my boy," declared the uncle, "it is not at all a bad-looking house. Evidently it has not been lived in for a long time. It's obviously been neglected, but it's possible that there are not many repairs to be made inside."

"In any case, the garden is very fine."

"Yes, the grounds are large enough. And what I like best is its wonderful seclusion. The wall surrounding it on all sides is very high, and the entrance gate would be hard for robbers to tackle."

"Shall I ring?"

"Yes, ring."

The young man pressed the button, and a peal rang out in the distance. Soon the caretaker appeared. He was a big fellow with long whiskers and a distinguished air, a model of the high-class servant.

"You gentlemen have come to see the house?"

"Exactly. I am Monsieur Durant. It is I who wrote to you."

"Yes sir. I remember."

The caretaker showed the two visitors into the garden, and as the uncle drew his nephew along the paths, the sense of proprietorship came over him at once, and he waxed knowledgeable.

"You see, Emile, it isn't big, but still it is amply sufficient. No trees in front of the house, which allows a view of the boulevard from all the windows. The servants' quarters, being in the far part of the garden, can in no way annoy the people in the house. Notice, too, that the trees are quite young and their foliage thin. I don't care for a garden that is too luxuriant; it's apt to block the view."

"That's right, Uncle."

The caretaker, who was following the two men, broke in upon the ecstasy of the prospective owner.

"Would you gentlemen like to see the house?"

"Certainly, certainly."

Before entering, however, M. Durant was bent on going around it. He noticed the smallest details, growing more and more enthusiastic.

"Look, Emile, it is very well built. The ground floor is sufficiently raised so as not to be too damp. This big terrace, on which the three French windows open, must be very cheerful in summer. Oh, there are drainpipes at the four corners! And we mustn't fail to see the cellars. I'm sure they're very fine. Bend down over the vents. What do you think of the gratings that close them? And, now, shall we go in?"

The caretaker led them to the main entrance.

"Here is the vestibule, gentlemen; to the left, the servants' hall and kitchen; to the right, the dining room; facing you, a small drawing room, then the large drawing room, and, last, the double staircase leading to the first floor."

The stout man dropped into a chair.

"And to whom does this place belong?"

"Lady Beltham, sir."

"She does not live here?"

"Not now. At the moment she is traveling."

With the caretaker as guide, uncle and nephew went through the rooms on the ground floor. As happens in all uninhibited houses, the damp had taken its toll. The flooring, worm-eaten, creaked under their feet, the carpets had large damp spots on them, the paper hung loose on the walls, while the furniture was covered with a thick coat of dust.

"Don't pay attention to the furniture, Emile; it's not important. What we must first look at is the arrangement of the rooms. Why, there are iron shutters—I like that."

"Yes, they are very practical."

"Yes, yes. To begin with, it will be impossible to see anything in the rooms from the outside when the shutters are closed. Not even the least light."

The caretaker proceeded to show them the first floor of the house.

"There is only one staircase?" asked the stout man.

"Yes, only one."

"And what is the cause of the unusual dampness? We are far from the Seine, and the garden is not very leafy."

"There is a leaky cistern in the cellar, sir. Here is the largest bedroom. It was my lady's."

"Yes. I can see it was the last room to be lived in."

At this harmless remark the caretaker seemed visibly upset.

"What makes you think that, sir?"

"Why, the chairs are pushed about as though they've recently been used. There is much less dust on the furniture. And . . . there's a print . . . look at the desk; there is a trace of dust on the diary. The blotting paper has been moved lately; someone has been writing there . . . why, what's wrong with you?"

As he listened to the stout man's remarks the caretaker grew strangely pale.

"Oh," he stammered, "it's nothing, nothing at all."

"But you seem afraid."

"Afraid? No, sir. I am not afraid . . . only—"

"Only what?"

"Well, gentlemen, it is best not to stay here. Lady Beltham is selling the house because it is . . . haunted!"

Neither of the visitors seemed impressed by this piece of information. The elder gentleman laughed loudly.

"Are there ghosts, then?"

"Yes sir. Spirits come here."

"Have you seen them?"

"Oh! Certainly not, sir. When they are here I shut myself up in the lodge. I can assure you—"

"When do they appear?"

"They almost always come on Tuesday nights."

And warming to his subject the caretaker gave details. He had first got the impression on one occasion when her ladyship was absent. She had left some days before for Italy. This happened on a Sunday, and then on Tuesday night while walking in the garden he heard movements inside the house.

"I went to fetch my keys and when I came back I found nobody! At first I thought it was burglars, but nothing had been taken. Yet I was not mistaken; furniture had been moved; there were bread crumbs on the floor."

The young man roared with laughter.

"Bread crumbs! Then your spirits come and sup here?"

The uncle, equally amused, asked: "And what did Lady Beltham think when you told her this story?"

"Lady Beltham laughed at me. But I had my own ideas. I watched in the garden daily and I heard the same sounds, and always on Tuesday nights. At last I laid a trap. I put a chalk mark around the chairs in Lady Beltham's room, she being still away. Well, sir, when I came to the house again on Thursday the chairs had been moved. I told Lady Beltham, and this time she seemed very frightened. It was then that she made up her mind to sell the house."

"For all that, what makes you say they are spirits?"

"What else could it be, sir. I also heard the sound of chains jangling. One night I even heard a strange, terrible hiss."

"Well!" cried the stout man, beginning to go down the staircase, "since the house is haunted I expect to pay less for it. Eh, Emile?"

"You will buy, sir, in spite of everything?"

"Of course. I find your phantoms less disturbing than the damp."

"Oh, the damp? That can be easily remedied. You will see that we have a central heating stove."

The caretaker led his visitors down a narrow stair to the cellar.

"Be careful, gentlemen. The stairs are slippery."

Then he observed, "You don't need a candle, the gratings are big enough to let in plenty of light."

"What is that?" asked the young man, pointing to a huge iron cylinder embedded in the earth and rising some four and a half feet above the floor.

"The cistern I mentioned. As you can see for yourselves, it is all but full."

The caretaker hurried on.

"That is the heating stove. There are conductors throughout the house. When it is in full blast the house is even too warm."

"But your grate stove is in pieces!" objected the stout man, pointing with his stick to iron plates torn out of one side of the central furnace.

"Oh, that happened at the time of the floods. But it won't cost much to put it right. If you gentlemen will examine the inside of the apparatus you will see that the pipes are in perfect order."

The uncle followed the caretaker's suggestion.

"Your pipes are as big as chimneys; a man could pass through them."

The inspection over, uncle and nephew bestowed a liberal tip on their guide. They would think it over and write or come again soon.

The two relatives retraced their steps to the boulevard Inkermann.

"Fandor?"

"Juve?"

"We have them!"

Uncle and nephew—that is to say, Juve and Fandor—could talk quite freely now.

"Juve, are you sure we have them this time?"

Juve pushed his friend into a bistro and ordered drinks. He then drew a blank sheet of paper from his pocket.

"What's that?"

"A piece of paper I picked up on Lady Beltham's desk when the caretaker's back was turned. It will serve for a little experiment. We should be able to find some fingerprints if anyone has touched it."

"On a blank piece of paper?"

"Yes, Fandor. Look!"

Juve took a pencil from his pocket and scratched off a fine dust of graphite that he shook over the paper. Gradually the outline of a hand appeared, faint, but quite visible.

"That's how," resumed Juve "With this very simple process, you can decipher the fingerprints of anyone who has written or rested his hands on anything—paper, glass, even wood. According to the clarity of this outline, which is made—thanks to the natural moisture of the hand—by the coagulation of the graphite which was laid on the paper, I can assure you that someone wrote on Lady Beltham's desk about ten days ago."

"That's wonderful," said Fandor. "Here, then, is proof positive that her ladyship visits her house from time to time."

"Correct—or at least that someone goes there. This is a man's hand."

"Well, Juve, what are you going to do now?"

"Now? I'm off to the prefecture to get rid of my padding, which bothers me no end. I've never been so glad that I'm not naturally chubby."

Fandor laughed. "I admit that I won't be sorry to get rid of my false mustache," he added. "The whole time I was inspecting that damned house, it kept tickling my nose and making me want to sneeze."

"You should have done so."

"And risk losing my mustache?"

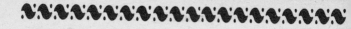

31

Lovers and Accomplices

"**W**ho's there?"

From the shadow came someone who calmly replied, "It's me."

"Ah! I know you now, but why the disguise?"

"Madame Superior, I present myself—Doctor Chaleck. Isn't my disguise as good as yours?"

"What do you want? You frighten me."

"To begin with, I thank you for returning at last to your house—our house. For five Tuesdays I have waited in vain. But first, Madame, explain your sudden conversion, the reason you've suddenly decided to take Orders. That's strange behavior for the mistress of Gurn."

Doctor Chaleck held under the lash of his irony the unhappy woman who seemed overcome by anxiety. The two were facing each other in the large room that formed the middle of the first floor of the house in the boulevard Inkermann at Neuilly. It was, in fact, the only room fit to be used. The other rooms in the elegant mansion had all gone to wrack and ruin.

It was here that the tragic drama had been played. Death had laid its cold hand upon the gilded trappings of the great house, and laughter and joy had taken flight. However, time passes so quickly and evil memories so soon grow dim that many had forgotten the grim happenings that three years earlier had beset the mansion on the boulevard.

First there was the deep mourning of Lady Beltham, whose husband had been mysteriously murdered at Belleville. Then, some weeks later, there was the awful scene of the arrest of Lord Beltham's murderer just as he was leaving the house—an arrest due to Juve, who, though he succeeded in apprehending the assassin, the infamous Gurn, was not able to prove (however sure he was) that the husband's murderer was the wife's lover.

After these shocking events Lady Beltham left France, dismissing the many attendants with whom she loved to surround herself like a true queen of beauty, luxury, and wealth. At rare intervals the lady, whose existence grew more and more mysterious, went back to her house at Neuilly for a few days. She would vanish, then reappear, living like a recluse, almost in entire solitude, receiving none of her old acquaintances.

About a year ago she seemed to want to settle at the boulevard Inkermann again. Workmen began to put the house in order; the lodge was opened and a family of caretakers arrived. Then suddenly the work was broken off. Weeks went by while Lady Beltham lived alone with her companion; then they both disappeared.

Now Lady Beltham shivered, and, gathering about her shoulders the cloak that covered her religious habit, she muttered: "I'm cold."

"Rotten weather, and to think this is July."

Chaleck crossed to a grille in the corner of the room.

"No good to leave that open!" he said. "An icy wind comes through the passage to the cellar."

Lady Beltham turned toward her enigmatic companion in alarm.

"Why did you let everyone think I was dead?"

"Why did you yourself leave here two days before the crime at the Cité Frochot?"

Lady Beltham hung her head, confessed, with a sob in her voice: "I was deserted and jealous. Besides, I was beginning to feel so remorseful. The idea had come to me to write down the terrible secret that haunted my spirit, to give the story to someone I could trust . . . an attorney, and then—"

"Go on!"

"And, then, what I had written suddenly vanished. It was then that I lost my head and fled. I have long wanted to withdraw from the world. The sisters of St. Clotilde offered to receive me in their house at Nogent."

Chaleck added brutally, "That isn't all. You forgot to say you were afraid. Come, be frank; afraid of Gurn, of me!"

"Well, yes. I was afraid. Not so much of you, but of our crimes. I am also afraid of dying."

"That confession you wrote became known to someone who confided it to me."

"Heavens," murmured the unhappy woman. "Who was it?"

Chaleck had again crossed to the grille which, although closed by him some moments before, had opened again, letting into the room a blast of icy air from the basement.

"This can't stay shut, it must be seen to," he muttered.

Lady Beltham, shaking nervously, persisted: "Who betrayed me? Who told?"

Chaleck sat beside her.

"You remember Valgrand the actor? Well, Valgrand was married. His wife sought to clear up the mystery of his disappearance and went . . . where, I ask you? Why, to you, Lady Beltham! You took her as companion! It would have been impossible to introduce a more redoubtable spy into the house than the widow Valgrand, known by you under the name of Madame Raymond."

Lady Beltham was panic-stricken.

"We are lost!"

Chaleck squeezed her two hands in a genuine burst of affection.

"We are saved!" he shouted. "Madame Raymond will talk no more!"

"The body at the Cité Frochot!"

Chaleck nodded. "Yes."

She looked at him with a mixture of repulsion and horror.

"Now, understand that that death saved you, and if I saved you it is because I loved you, love you still, will always love you!"

Lady Beltham, overcome, allowed herself to fall into Chaleck's arms, her head resting on her lover's shoulder as she wept hot tears. Once more she was enslaved, a captive! More than two years ago she had broken with the mysterious and terrible being whom she had once incited to kill her husband, and with whom she then committed the most appalling of crimes. During this separation the unhappy woman had tried to pull herself together, to acquire a fresh honesty of mind and body, a new soul. She dreamed of finding in religion some help, some forgetfulness. She had later experienced the frightful tortures of jealousy, knowing that her former lover had mistresses! But she resisted the temptation to see him again, and pictured him to herself in such a terrible guise that she felt an overwhelming fear of finding herself face to face with him. Now the season of calm and quiet she had evoked was suddenly dispelled. First came the mysterious disappearance of her confession and the horrible crime of the Cité Frochot. To be sure, she did not then know that Doctor Chaleck, of whom the papers spoke, was none other than Gurn. But hadn't *The Capital* spoken of Fantômas in that connection? And at this disquieting comparison Lady Beltham felt a sinister foreboding. Other mysteries had then supervened, unknown to the guilty lady, who by that time was already seeking her new birth in the bosom of religion. Her miseries would soon grow definite enough.

At the very gate of the convent an innocent man, Bonardin, the actor, fell victim to the attack of Juve, who was also innocent. In that affair she felt the complicity of her former lover growing more and more certain. She then received a letter from him, followed by others. Gurn summoned her to his place—their place—the mansion at Neuilly, every Tuesday night. She held out several times despite his threat of reprisals. But at last she yielded and went. She had expected Gurn, but it was Chalek she found. The two were one and the same!

Now she was faced with this accomplice, guilty of new crimes, clothed in a new personality, already under suspicion, which doubtless he would cast off only to assume another that would enable him to extend still further the list of his crimes! But despite all the horror her lover inspired in her, she felt herself tamed again, powerless to resist him, ready to do anything the moment he bade her!

She asked feebly, "Who was it killed Madame Raymond?

Was it that thief whom they speak of in the papers—
Loupart?''

''Well, not exactly!''

''Then was it you? Tell me, I would rather know.''

''It was neither he nor I, and yet it was to some extent
both of us.''

''I do not understand.''

''It is rather difficult to understand. Our 'executioner' does
not lack originality. I may say it is something that lives yet
does not think.''

''Who is it! Who is it!''

''Why not ask Inspector Juve? Oh! Juve, too, would like
to know who all these people are. Gurn, Chaleck, Loupart,
and, above all—Fantômas!''

''Fantômas! Ah, I dare not utter that name. And yet a
doubt oppresses my heart! Tell me, are you not, yourself—
Fantômas?''

Chaleck freed himself gently, for Lady Beltham had wound
her arms around his neck.

''I know nothing. I am merely the lover who loves you.''

''Then let us go far away. Let us begin a new life together.
Will you? Come!'' She stopped suddenly. ''I heard a noise.''
Chaleck, too, listened. Some slight creakings had, indeed,
disturbed the hush of the room. But outside the wind and the
rain whirled around the dilapidated, lonely abode, and it was
not surprising that unaccountable sounds should be audible
in the stillness. Once more Lady Beltham built up her plans,
catching a glimpse of a future filled with peace and happi-
ness.

With a brief, harsh remark, Chaleck brought her back to
reality.

''All that cannot be, at least for the moment, we must
first—''

Lady Beltham laid her hand on his lips.

''Do not speak!'' she begged. ''A fresh crime—that's what
you mean?''

''A vengeance, an execution! A man has set himself to run
me down, has sworn my ruin. Between us it is a struggle
without mercy; my life is not safe but at the cost of his, so
he must perish. In four days they will find Detective Juve

dead in his own bed. And with him will finally vanish the fiction he has evoked of Fantômas! Fantômas! Ah, if society knew . . . if humanity, instead of being what it is . . . but it doesn't matter!''

"And Fantômas? What will become of him—and you?"

"Did I say that I was Fantômas?"

"No," she stammered, "but—"

The dim light of a pale dawn filtered past the closed shutters of the large drawing room in which lover and mistress had met again, after long weeks of separation, to evoke sinister memories. For all their hopes the limit of the tribulations to which they were prey still seemed far away.

Chaleck blew out the lamp, drew the curtains aside, and sharply put an end to their meeting.

"I'm off, Lady Beltham. Soon we shall meet again. Never let anyone suspect what we have said to each other. Farewell."

The hapless woman, crushed and broken by emotion, remained alone in the great room for nearly an hour. Then the demands of her official life reasserted themselves. It was necessary to return to the convent at Nogent.

Extricating themselves painfully from the pipes of the great stove, Juve and Fandor, covered with plaster, wreathed with cobwebs, and sprinkled with dust, fell back suddenly into the middle of the cellar. The two men, oblivious to the disarray of their dress and their painfully cramped limbs, spoke at once, dumbfounded but joyful.

"Well, Juve?"

"Well, Fandor, we got something for our money."

"Oh, what a lovely night, Juve. I wouldn't have given up my place for a fortune."

"We had front seats, though to be sure the velvet armchairs were lacking."

They were silent for a moment, their minds fully occupied with a crowd of ideas. So Chaleck and Loupart were one and the same? And Lady Beltham was indeed the accomplice of Gurn. An unhappy accomplice, repentant, wretched, a criminal through love.

"Fandor, we have them now. Let's make our move!"

The pair, not sorry to breathe a little more easily than they had done for the past few hours, went upstairs, reached the ground floor, and made their way into the drawing room, where during the night Doctor Chaleck and Lady Beltham had had their memorable reunion.

Juve, without a word, paced up and down the room, poking in all the corners, then gave a cry: "Here is the mouth of the heater that brute Chaleck tried to shut and I persisted in opening so as not to lose a word he was saying. So what if he felt cold, what did I feel like?"

"The fact is," added Fandor, whose voice had grown hoarse from his recent ordeal, "these stove pipes have very little comfort about them."

"What did you expect?" asked Juve. "The architect wasn't thinking of us when he built the house. Now, Fandor, we have a hard job ahead of us, and we need all the luck we can get. For certainly it is Fantômas we have unearthed: Fantômas, the lover of Lady Beltham, the slayer of her husband, the murderer of Valgrand, the master who did away with Madame Raymond! Gurn, Chaleck, Loupart. The one being who can be all those and himself too—Fantômas."

As the two friends quietly left Lady Beltham's house, the detective drew from his pocket a kind of fish scale that he showed to Fandor.

"What do you make of this?"

"I haven't the least idea."

"Well, I have, and it may lead us right to a great discovery. Did you notice that Chaleck didn't say definitely who the executioner of Madame Raymond was?"

"Absolutely."

"Well, I believe I have a morsel of this 'executioner' in my pocket.

32
The Silent Executioner

J uve was in his study smoking a cigarette. It was nine in the evening. The door leading to the lobby opened and Fandor walked in.

"All right, this evening?"

"All right. What brings you here, Fandor?"

The journalist smiled and pointed to a calendar on the wall. "The fact that . . . it's this evening, Juve."

"The date fixed by Chaleck or Fantômas for my demise. Tomorrow morning I'm to be found in my bed, strangled, crushed, or something of the sort. I suppose you've come to get a farewell interview for *The Capital*. To gather the minutest details of the frightful crime so that you can publish a special edition. 'THE TRAGEDY IN THE RUE BONAPARTE! JUVE OVERCOME BY FANTÔMAS!' "

Fandor listened, amused at the detective's outburst.

"You'd be angry with me, Juve," he declared in the same spirit, "for not taking advantage of such a sensational piece of news, wouldn't you?"

"That's right. And then I admit that I expected my last evening to be a lonely one, there was a feeling of sadness at the bottom of my heart. I thought that before dying I should have liked to say farewell to young Fandor, whose life I am continually putting in peril by my crazy ventures, but whom I love as the surest of companions, the sagest of advisers, the most discreet of confidants."

161

Fandor was touched. With a spontaneous movement he sprang to the armchair in which Juve sat, and seized and wrung the detective's hands.

"What?"

"I'm staying with you. You don't suppose I'm going to leave you to spend the night alone?"

Juve, touched beyond measure by Fandor's words, seemed uncertain what his decision should be.

"I can't pretend, Fandor, that your presence is not agreeable, and I'm grateful to you for your sympathy; I knew I could count on you. But after all, we must look ahead and consider all contingencies. Fantômas may succeed! Now you know what my plan is. But if I should fail, I like to think that you would carry on the work as my successor and put an end to Fantômas."

"But, Juve, you are threatened by Fantômas. That's why I'm here to help you."

"Well, I have no bed to put you in."

Fandor, taken aback, stared at the detective. The latter rose and began to pace the room. Then he turned sharply and gazed at the young man.

"You are quite determined to stay with me?" he asked.

"Yes."

"And if I insist that you go?"

"I will disobey you."

"Very well, then," concluded Juve, shrugging his shoulders, "come along."

The detective went out of the room and headed for the stairs.

"Where are we bound for?" asked Fandor.

"The garret," Juve replied.

A quarter of an hour later Juve and Fandor dragged a huge open-work wicker basket into the bedroom.

"Whew!" cried Juve, mopping his forehead, "no one would believe it was so heavy."

Fandor smiled.

"It's full of rubbish. Really, Juve, you're not a neat man!"

Juve, without reply, proceeded to empty the basket, pulling out books, linen, pieces of wood, carpet, rolls of paper; in fact, the accumulated refuse of fifteen years.

"How tall are you?" he asked.

"Five foot ten."

Juve got out his pocket measure and took the length of the crate.

"That's all right," he murmured. "You'll be quite snug and comfortable in it."

Fandor exclaimed, "You're a cheerful host, Juve. You bottle up your guests in cages now!"

Juve placed a mattress at the bottom of the basket and laid two blankets over that. Then he put a pillow on top. Patting the bedding to make it smooth, he declared with a laugh: "I fear nothing, but I have taken precautions. Two men have been posted in the caretaker's lodge. My revolver is loaded, and I've dined comfortably. At about half-past eleven I shall go to bed as usual. However, instead of going to sleep I'll try to stay awake. At dinner I took three cups of coffee, and when you go I shall drink a fourth."

"Excuse me," said Fandor, "but I am not going away."

"There! You'll sleep splendidly inside that, Fandor."

The journalist, used to his friend's devices, nodded his head. Juve had already taken off his coat and vest, and now pulled from a box three belts half a yard wide and studded with sharp points. "Look, Fandor! I shall be completely protected when I am swathed in them. Oh," he added, "I almost forgot my leg guards!"

Juve went back to the box and took out two more rolls, also studded with spikes. Fandor looked at this gear in amazement.

"It will cost me a pair of sheets and maybe a mattress," Juve said, laughing.

"How does it work?"

"They have a double object: to protect me against Fantômas, or the executioner he will send, and also to allow me to determine the civil status of the executioner in question."

Fandor, growing more puzzled, inspected the iron spikes, which were two inches or more in length.

"It's not a new device," said Juve. "Liabeuf wore arm guards like these under his jacket, and when the officers wanted to seize him they tore their hands."

"I know, I know," replied Fandor, "but—"

Suddenly the detective touched a finger to his lips.

"It's now twenty past eleven, and I'm in the habit of going to bed at half past. Fantômas is bound to know this. When he comes or sends, he must not notice anything out of the ordinary. Get into your wicker case and shut the lid carefully. By the way, I'm going to leave the window slightly open."

"Isn't that a bit risky?"

"It's also one of my habits, and I don't want to make Fantômas suspicious by doing anything different."

Fandor settled himself in his case and Juve also got into bed. As he put out the light he gave a warning.

"We mustn't close an eye or utter a word. Whatever happens, don't move. But when I call, turn on a light immediately and come to me."

"All right," said Fandor.

"Fandor!"

Juve's cry, loud and compelling, rent the stillness of the night. The journalist leaped from his wicker basket so abruptly that he knocked against the lamp stand and the lamp fell to the floor. Fandor searched for his matches in vain.

"Light up, Fandor!" shouted Juve.

The noise of a struggle, the dull thud of something falling to the floor, maddened the journalist. In the darkness he heard Juve groaning, scraping the floor with his boots, making violent efforts to resist some mysterious assailant.

"Hurry, for God's sake," implored the agonized voice of the detective. Fandor then stepped on the glass of the lamp, breaking it. He tripped, knocked his head against a cupboard, rebounded, then suddenly cried out in terror. His hands, stretched apart in the gloom, had brushed a cold, shiny object that slid under his palms.

"Fandor! Help, Fandor!"

Desperate, Fandor plunged haphazard about the disordered room, wrapped in darkness. Suddenly he rushed into the adjoining study, found another lamp there, lit it quickly, and hurried back with it.

A fearful sight wrung a cry of terror from him. Juve, on his knees on the floor, was covered with blood.

"Juve!"

"It's all right, Fandor. It's someone else's blood, not mine."

The detective rushed to the open window and leaned out into the dark night.

"Listen!" he cried. "Do you hear that low hissing, that dull rustling?"

"Yes. I heard it just now."

"That was the executioner."

The detective drew back into the room, shut the window, pulled down the blinds, and then took off his armor. He examined the bloodstains and the tiny shreds of flesh that had remained on the points with great curiosity.

"We have no more to fear now," he said. "He's tried—and failed."

"Juve! tell me what just happened? I may be an idiot, but I don't understand at all!"

"You're no fool, Fandor, far from it, but while you reason and argue very astutely, you have far less deductive faculty. That does not seem to be your forte."

Fandor sat down in front of the detective, and the latter held forth.

"When we found ourselves faced with the first crime, that of the Cité Frochot, and our attention was drawn to the elusive Fantômas, we were unable to decide how poor Madame Raymond, whom we then took for Lady Beltham, had been killed. Now remember, Fandor, that during that night of mystery, hidden behind the curtains in Chaleck's study, we heard strange rustlings and a faint sort of hissing, didn't we?"

"We did," admitted Fandor, at a loss. "But go on, Juve."

"When we were called to investigate the attack on the American, Dixon, it was easy for us to conclude that the attempt on his life was the outcome of the same plan of battle that cost the widow Valgrand her life. The mysterious executioner, which Chaleck did not disguise from Lady Beltham, was therefore a being endowed with enough strength to completely crush a woman's body, and probably do as much to an ordinary man. But the executioner in question wasn't strong enough to subdue the champion boxer.

"This instrument of limited power, if I may so describe it, must then be, not a mechanism which nothing can resist, but a living being! It must also be a creature that arouses panic— terrifying, formidable. You ask why, Fandor?''

"Yes."

"I'm going to tell you. If our poor friend Josephine were not still in critical condition she would certainly support me. You remember the business on the boulevard Pereire? Chaleck or Fantômas wants to be rid of the woman he loved under the guise of Loupart, since he has gone back to Lady Beltham. Moreover, Josephine is too friendly with Dixon and with the police.

"Chaleck/Fantômas therefore goes up to Josephine's. After telling the poor girl I know not what yarn, he departs, leaving behind in his bag the instrument. Now this, when it shows itself, so terrifies the poor girl that she throws herself out of the window.''

"I'm beginning to see what you mean," said the journalist.

"Listen," said Juve. "The mysterious, nameless, and terrible accomplice of Fantômas is nothing more than a snake! A snake trained to crush bodies in its coils. I had long suspected its existence, but I began to be sure of it when I found that strange scale at Neuilly. This accounts for the incomprehensible condition of Madame Valgrand's body, the extraordinary attempt on Dixon, the murderous thing that terrified Josephine! That is why, expecting tonight's visit, I barbed myself with iron like a knight of old, feeling pretty sure that if the hands of the officers were torn by Liabeuf's armlets, the coils of Fantômas's serpent would be flayed on touching my sharp spikes.''

"Juve!" cried Fandor, "if I hadn't knocked over the lamp we would have caught this thing.''

"Probably, but what would we have done with it? After all, it's better for it to go back to Fantômas.''

"But you haven't told me what happened!''

The young man's face displayed such confusion that Juve couldn't help laughing.

"Journalist! Incorrigible newsmonger! All right, take notes for your article describing this appalling adventure. So, then, Fandor, once the lamp is out, the hours go by, a trifle more slowly in the darkness than in the light. You are silent and still as a little Moses in your wicker cradle. As for me, armored as I was, I tried not to stir in my bed—to spare the sheets. Juve is not wealthy. Midnight, one o'clock, two, quarter past. How slowly the time goes! Then, a noise! A cat that meows strangely. Then comes that little hissing sound I begin to know. Hiss—hiss! I guess that the window is opening wider. You heard, as I did, Fandor, the revolting scales grit on the boards. But you didn't know what it was, whereas I knew it was a snake! I swear to you, it took all my nerve not to flinch, but I wanted to see it through to the end at whatever cost, and know whether, behind this reptile, Fantômas wouldn't show his vile snout.

"Ah, the brute. How quickly he went to work. As I listened, my muscles tense, my nerves on edge, I suddenly felt the sheet stir—the foul beast is trained to attack beds, remember the attack on Dixon—and suddenly I felt its grip—furious, quick as a whip stroke—twining about me. I was thrown down, tossed, shaken, torn like a feather, tied up like a sausage!

"My arms were glued to my body, my loins hampered. I didn't intend to say a word; I had faith in my ironwork. But to be honest, I was scared, terribly scared. That's when I yelled: 'Fandor! Help!'

"Oh, those awful moments. It began to squeeze horribly when all at once I felt a cold liquid flow over my skin—blood. The brute was wounded. We still wrestled, and you tripped in the darkness and smashed the glass of the lamp, and I felt myself gradually choking. I'll remember it all my life. And then, what relief, when the grip slackens, when he gives up and makes off. The beast glided over the floor, reached the window, hissed frantically, and vanished. There, Monsieur Reporter, you have impressions from life, and tough ones, too! Well, the luck is turning, and I think it's veering to our side. Things are going from bad to worse for Fantômas. I tell you, Fandor, we'll have him before long!''

33
A Scandal in
the Cloister

Slight sounds, barely audible, disturbed the peace of the cloister. In the deep silence of the night, vague noises could be distinguished. Furtive steps, whisperings, doors opened or shut cautiously. Then the blinking light of a candle shone at a casement, two or three other windows were illuminated, and the hubbub increased. Voices were heard, frightened interjections. Then the din increased in the long corridor on which the nuns' cells opened. Usually the curtains of these cells were discreetly drawn; now they were being pulled aside. Drowsy faces looked out of the gloom; the excitement increased.

"Sister Marguerite! Sister Vincent! Sister Clotilde! What is it? What is happening? Listen!"

The alarmed nuns gathered at the far end of the passage. The women, roused from their sleep, had hastily arranged their hair and wrapped themselves in their flowing robes. They turned their frightened faces toward the chapel.

"Burglars!" murmured the sister who was treasurer of the convent, thinking of the gold cup that the humble little sisterhood preserved as a relic.

The senior, Sister Vincent, quivering with alarm, stammered: "It is a revolution—I saw that in '70."

A pile of chairs under the vaulting suddenly toppled over. Panic-stricken, the sisters crowded close together, not daring to go to the chapel, which was connected to the passage by a little staircase.

And the mother superior, what did she think of it all—what would she say? They drew near the cell, a little apart from the others, occupied by the lady, who, on taking the headship of the house, had brought with her precious personal effects and a good deal of money as well. Sister Vincent, who had gone forward and was about to enter the little chamber, drew back.

"Our holy mother," she informed the others, "is at prayer."

At this very moment broken cries rang through the passage. Sister Françoise, the caretaker, who everyone believed was calmly sleeping in her lodge, suddenly appeared, her eyes wild, her garments in disarray.

The sisters gathered around her, but the helpless woman shrieked, quite beside herself.

"Let me go! Let us flee! I have seen the devil! He is there! In the church! It is frightful!"

Mad with terror, the sister explained in disjointed phrases what had alarmed her. She had heard a noise and thought it might be the gardener's dog shut in the chapel by mistake. Then behold! The moment she entered the choir the stained-glass window above the shrine of St. Clotilde, their patroness, suddenly gave way, and through the opening appeared a supernatural being who came toward her, exclaiming words she could not understand. Armed with a huge club, he struck right and left, making a terrible uproar.

Then the caretaker made an effort to escape, but the demon barred her path, and in a sepulchral voice commanded her to go for the mother superior and bid her come at once, if she did not want the worst of evils to befall the sisterhood.

She had barely finished when an echoing crash was heard. The sisters suppressed a cry, and as they turned, pale with dread, they saw before them their mother superior. With a sweeping gesture she vaguely gave a blessing as if to endow them with courage, then turned to the caretaker.

"My dear Sister Françoise, calm yourself! Be brave! God will not forsake us! I intend to comply with the stranger's wishes. I will go alone—with God alone!" Lady Beltham made a mighty effort to disguise the emotion she felt. Slowly she went down the steps and entered the sanctuary, where she stopped in terror.

The choir stall was lit up. Candles were flaring on the high altar, and in the middle of the chapel, wrapped in a large black cloak, his face hidden by a black mask, stood a man, mysterious and alarming.

"Lady Beltham!"

At the sound of this voice, Lady Beltham thought she recognized her lover.

"What do you want? What are you doing? This is madness!"

"Nothing is madness in Fantômas!"

Lady Beltham pressed her hands to her heart, unable to speak.

The voice went on: "Fantômas bids you leave here, Lady Beltham. In two hours you will go from this convent; a closed car will be waiting for you at the back of the garden, at the little gate. The vehicle will take you to a seaport, where you will board a vessel that will be indicated by the driver; when the voyage is over you will be in England. There you will receive fresh orders to head for Canada."

Lady Beltham wrung her hands in despair.

"Why do you force me to leave my dear companions?"

"Were you not ready to leave everything, Lady Beltham, to make a new life for yourself with . . . him you love?"

"Alas!"

"Remember last Tuesday night at the Neuilly mansion!"

"Ah! You should have carried me off then, not left me time to think it over. Now I am no longer willing."

"You will go! Yes or no? Will you obey?"

"I will—for, after all, I love you!"

The two tragic beings were silent for a moment, listening. Outside the church the uproar grew in violence. Brief orders were being shouted, whistles rang out. Suddenly, uttering a hoarse cry, the villain exclaimed: "The police! The police are on the track of Fantômas! Juve's police. Well, this time Fantômas will be too much for them. Lady Beltham—till we meet again."

Beating a rapid retreat behind a pillar of the chapel he

vanished. Lady Beltham found herself alone in the chapel.
Five minutes later the heavy steps of the police sounded in
the passages. They went through the house, searching for
clues, then disappeared in the darkness of the night.

Lady Beltham addressed the nuns:

"A great peril threatens our sisters of the boulevard Jourdan. They must be warned at all costs and at once. And it is
necessary that I, and I only, should go to warn them. Have
no fear. No harm will come to me. I know what I am doing."

Under the appalled eyes of the sisterhood the mother superior slowly passed from the assembled community with a
sweeping gesture of farewell. The moment she was alone,
she ran to the far end of the garden and left through the little
gate in the wall behind the chapel. She was gone!

While these strange occurrences were in progress at the
peaceful convent of Nogent, and the flight of Lady Beltham
at the bidding of Fantômas was effected under the eyes of the
sisters, nothing stirred in the environs of La Chapelle, in the
dreaded region where the hooligans of the celebrated Cyphers
have their haunts.

A certain anarchy reigned in the confederation, due to the
fact that Loupart had not been seen for some time. None of
its members believed for an instant the newspaper story that
Loupart had turned out to be Fantômas—the elusive, the su-
perhuman, the improbable, the mysterious Fantômas. This
was beyond them. Well enough to stuff the numbskulls of the
law with such a tale, but the members of the Cyphers had no
use for such drivel.

That same evening there was considerable excitement at
the station in the rue Stephenson. Detectives, inspectors, and
hooligans—real or sham—were assembled there.

"Who is that gentleman?" asked M. Rouquelet, the superintendent of the district, pointing to a young man seated
in a corner of the room, taking notes on a pad.

Juve, to whom the question was addressed, turned his head.

"Why, it's Fandor, Jerôme Fandor, my friend."

Juve was seated at the magistrate's table, comparing papers, documents, and material evidence; he had, standing
around him, uniformed men or plainclothesmen. One might

have thought it was the office of a general staff during battle. The door opened to a man dressed like a market gardener.

"Well, Léon?" asked Juve.

"Monsieur Inspector, we've done it. We've nabbed the Cooper."

A sergeant of the nineteenth arrondissement appeared and saluted.

"Sir, my men are bringing in The Flirt. Her throat has been cut."

"Is her attacker in custody?"

"Not yet—there are several of them—but we know them. The wounded woman was able to tell us their names. They cut her because they suspected her of giving us information."

M. Rouquelet telephoned to Lâriboisière for an ambulance, and the officers went to see the victim, who was lying on a stretcher in the hall. At that moment the sound of a struggle caused Juve to hurry to the entrance of the station. Some officers were hauling in a youth with a pallid complexion and wicked eyes. Fandor recognized the captive.

"It's that little student who bit my finger the night of the Marseilles express!"

Léon, who had drawn near, likewise identified the youth.

"I know him; that's Mimile. His goose is cooked!"

The hall of the station filled once more. An old woman, dragged in forcibly, was groaning and bawling at the top of her lungs: "Pack of swine! Aren't you ashamed to treat a poor woman so!"

"We caught this woman, Mother Toulouche, in the act of hiding in her corsette a bundle of bank notes just passed to her by a man," explained one of the men. "Here they are."

The constable handed the packet to the judge, and Fandor, who was watching, could not repress an exclamation.

"Oh! Notes in halves! I suppose they belong to Monsieur Martialle! Allow me, Monsieur Rouquelet, to look at the numbers."

"In with Mother Toulouche!" cried the superintendent; then rubbing his hands he turned to Juve and added: "A fine haul, Juve. What do you think?"

But Juve didn't hear him. He had drawn Fandor into a corner of the office and was explaining: "I have done no more at present than have Lady Beltham shadowed, but I do not mean to arrest her. You see, if I asked Fuselier for a warrant against Lady Beltham, someone legally dead and buried more than two months ago, that excellent functionary would swallow his clerk, stool and all, in sheer amazement.''

At that moment a cyclist constable, dripping with sweat and quite out of breath, came in and went directly to Juve.

"I come from Nogent!" he cried.

"Well?"

"Well, sir, they saw a masked man come out of the convent wrapped in a big cloak. They gave chase—he fired a revolver twice and killed two officers."

"Good God! It was certainly—"

"We thought, too . . . that perhaps . . . after all . . . it was . . . it was Fantômas!"

"Juve!" called the commissioner. "You are wanted on the telephone. Neuilly is asking for you."

The detective picked up the receiver.

"Hello! hello! Is that you, Michel? Yes. What is it? In a car? Oh, you have taken the driver. But he—damn it! Who the devil is this man who always escapes us? What? He is in Lady Beltham's house! You have surrounded the house? Good, keep your eyes open! Do nothing till I come."

Juve hung up the receiver and turned to Fandor.

"Fantômas is at Lady Beltham's, shut up in the house. I'm going there."

"I'll go with you."

As the two men left the station they were met by Inspector Grolle.

"We have taken The Beard at Daddy Korn's," he cried.

"Confound that!" shouted Juve, as he jumped into a taxi with Fandor. "Neuilly! Boulevard Inkermann, and hurry!"

34
Fantômas's Revenge

"**P**hew! Here I am!"

Checking his headlong course at the top of the steps, Fantômas rapidly entered the house, then double-locked himself in. The villain immediately inspected the fastenings of the windows and doors on the ground floor.

The monster cocked his ear. A horn sounded dolefully three times in the silence of the night. Fantômas counted them anxiously and then exclaimed: "There! That's my signal! My driver has been taken."

A slight shudder shook the man's sturdy frame. He went up to the first floor and peered through the shutters. He caught the sound of footsteps. In the light of a streetlamp he suddenly spied the outline of his driver. The latter, among a group of policemen, was walking, head bent, with his hands cuffed.

"Poor fellow!" he murmured. "Another who has to pay! But there's no time to lose, I'll bet that Juve, flanked by his everlasting journalist, will soon be here. Very well! Juve it is not as master that you will enter this house but as a doomed man!"

Fantômas now became engrossed in a strange task that absorbed all his attention. On the floor of the dark closet where all the electric gear of the house terminated, the villain

174

laid a sort of oblong fuse that he drew from his capacious cloak.

To the end of this fuse he attached two electric wires previously removed from their insulation. Then, having verified the tie of the pulls of the distribution board, he hid the cartridge under a little wooden lid. Then he left the closet, taking care to double-lock the door.

"These detectives," he growled, "are about to witness the finest fireworks display imaginable and, I dare say, take part in it, too. Dynamite can transform a respectable middle-class house into a sparkling bouquet of loose stone!"

If Juve and Fandor had paid more attention to the piping of the wires, they would have seen that some of them ran outside the house and disappeared below ground, reappearing in an old deserted woodshed at the far end of the property.

Fantômas was about to leave the house. He was already stepping onto the terrace when, suppressing a curse, he wheeled about suddenly.

As Juve and Fandor were about to enter the grounds, Detective Michel rose up out of the dusk.

"That you, sir?"

"Well," replied Juve, "is the bird in the nest?"

"Yes, sir, and the cage is well guarded, I assure you. Fifteen of my men are keeping a strict watch on the house."

"Good. Here is the plan of action. You, sergeant, will enter the house with Inspector Michel, at my back. The men will continue to watch the exit."

Juve broke off sharply. He saw the door of the house open a little and Fantômas appear, then vanish again inside the house.

"At last!" cried Juve, who sprang forward, followed by Fandor.

"Slowly, gentleman! Victory is now in sight; we mustn't be rash. You remain on the ground floor, each one in a room, and don't move without good reason. I'm going up."

"I'm going with you," exclaimed Fandor.

The two cautiously went up the stairs to the first floor.

"Fantômas!" challenged Juve, stopping on the landing, "we have you; surrender!"

But the detective's voice only roused distant echoes; the big house was silent.

"Now, this is what we must do," he cautioned Fandor. "Above us is a loft—we will search it first; if it's empty, we'll close it again. Then we'll come down again, taking each room in turn and locking it after us. At the slightest sound, throw yourself on the ground and let Fantômas fire first; the flash of the shot will tell us where he is."

The two manhunters searched the loft without success. At the first floor Juve repressed a slight tremor, for the handle of the door leading into Lady Beltham's room creaked ominously. He opened it, jumping aside quickly, expecting to be fired at. The room was empty; there was no trace of Fantômas. The two passed into another room, then, as soon as their search was complete, locked up that area.

Suddenly, as they reached the foot of the stairs, Juve gave a violent start. From the door of the drawing room a shadow, black from head to foot, came bounding out. Quick as lightning the form crossed the anteroom, then plunged through a low entrance into the cellar. Suddenly, two shots rang out.

Fantômas drew a big bar behind him and prided himself on the barrier he had put between his pursuers and himself. But despite his consummate confidence, he was beginning to feel a certain uneasiness, an undeniable anxiety. His black mask clung to his temples, dripping with sweat.

He crossed the basement to the little vent overlooking the garden.

"That is a way of escape," he thought. "Unless—"

But, baffled, he stopped speculating.

"Damn it! There are three policemen at that exit."

He lit a match and reviewed the place in which he found himself, which for that matter he knew better than any one there. Facing him stood the dilapidated stove, and at his feet the cistern shimmered. Suddenly Fantômas clenched his fists. Under the increasing blows of the detective and his men, the door of the basement began to give way. Above the crash of the boards and ironwork Juve's voice rang out:

"Fantômas! Surrender!"

Fantômas groped in the darkness. His hand touched a bottle. A crackle of shattered glass was heard. Fantômas had taken the bottle by the neck and broken it against the wall.

Juve, revolver in hand, followed by Fandor, moved cautiously down the stairs to the cellar. They felt their hearts beating as though they would burst.

Juve reached the last step. He pressed the knob of his flashlight; a small glow lit the little room. It was empty!

Juve went around the cellar, carefully inspecting the walls and sounding them with the butt of his revolver. He went around the cistern. Its surface was black and still. A broken bottle, floating head downward, remained half immersed, absolutely motionless.

Fandor laid his hand on the detective's arm.

"Did you hear; someone breathed!"

"Idiots that we are! He's in there," cried Juve, pointing to the pipe of the great stove.

The detective caught sight of a few bundles of straw in a corner.

"That's what we want, Fandor! We're going to make a bonfire."

When the opening of the furnace was fitted, Juve ignited it and the flames rose, crackling, while a pungent smoke, thick and black, rose up the pipe heater.

"And now to the opening of the stove! Sergeant! Michel! This way!"

Through the apertures in the ground-floor rooms the great stove was beginning to smoke.

A broken bottle with the bottom gone was floating head downward on the black water of the tank. Juve and Fandor had barely gone when the water stirred, and slowly, the mysterious bottle rose to the top again. Behind it rose the head of Fantômas, still wrapped in the black hood that now clung to his face like a mask molded on the features.

Dripping, he emerged from the tank and breathed hard for a few minutes. Despite this ingenious contrivance for feeding his lungs, he was not far from suffocating.

"All the same," he thought, "if I hadn't remembered the plan of the Tonkingese who lie stretched at the bottom of a river for hours at a time, breathing through hollow reeds, I think this time we should have exchanged shots to some purpose!''

Fantômas was wringing out his clothes when loud cries sounded above his head, and two or three shots rang out. At the same time, there was a sudden stirring in and around the house. He turned it to account by going to the vent immediately. There was no one on guard now, so Fantômas put his head through, then his shoulders.

''That's all right; the brute's dead!''

Juve was curiously examining the creature who lay helpless on the floor. Two trembling sergeants stood at the door of the room.

''We were expecting Fantômas to appear, and a snake unrolls itself and springs in our faces!'' cried Fandor.

Half emerging from the mouth of the heater the monstrous body of a boa constrictor lay on the floor. The men Juve had brought into the house were resolute, ready for anything, but never did they imagine that Fantômas could assume such an unexpected shape. And terrified and overwhelmed with dread, they recoiled in a frenzy of fear and fled, calling on their mates outside, who ran to their assistance.

''Sir!'' A terrified voice called from outside.

Juve rushed to the window. A dripping creature, clad in black from head to foot, crossed the garden, running toward the servants' quarters. It was Fantômas. Juve swore loudly. ''There he is! Getting away!''

The detective's cry was left unfinished.

As he emerged through the vent, Fantômas leaped forward. He was free!

''Juve scored the first game, the second is mine,'' he cried.

He reached the woodshed. With a practiced hand he pulled the switch, igniting a spark in the dark closet behind the pantry.

''I win!'' shouted Fantômas, as a terrible explosion sounded.

The earth shook, a huge column of black smoke rose skyward, and explosion followed explosion. The roar of walls collapsing was mingled with fearful cries and dying groans.

Lady Beltham's villa had been blown up, burying under its ruins the hapless men who had ventured too near in their pursuit of Fantômas. The archcriminal had escaped once more. But were Juve and Fandor among the dead?

About the Author

Marcel Allain and Pierre Souvestre published FANTÔMAS in 1911. It's astonishing success encouraged them to produce twenty sequels before Souvestre's death in 1914, after which Allain went on to write another eleven on his own (and marry Souvestre's widow).

BOUNCING BACK

How to Handle Setbacks in Your Work and Personal Life

ANDREW J. DuBRIN

PaperJacks LTD.

Toronto   New York

One of a series of books
published by PaperJacks Ltd.

BOUNCING BACK

How to Handle Setbacks in Your Work and Personal Life

To Drew

Published by arrangement with Prentice-Hall, Inc., Englewood Cliffs,
New Jersey 07632
Prentice-Hall edition published 1982

PaperJacks edition published September 1984

Second Printing August 1985

Cover design: Brant Cowie/Artplus Ltd.

This PaperJacks edition is printed from brand-new plates. No part of this book
may be reproduced or transmitted in any form or by any means, electronic or
mechanical, including photography, recording, or any information storage or
retrieval system, without permission in writing from Prentice-Hall, Inc.
PaperJacks editions are published by PaperJacks Ltd., 330 Steelcase Road East,
Markham, Ontario, Canada L3R 2M1.